REJECT

Benjamin and Isaiah

J.K. Anderson

PROLOGUE

Grace was feeling incredibly happy and ready to celebrate. After years of contemplating this decision, Grace's husband, Matthew, finally agreed. The two lovers quit their full-time time jobs, sold their small house, and were planning a move from California to Illinois in hopes of raising a large family with a big house and yard.

Grace packed her things, wide-eyed, with a smile growing on her face. Matthew watched his wife pack as if this new chapter in their life would bring nothing but joy. Matthew, on the other hand, wasn't so sure, yet who could say no to such a beautiful woman—especially while infatuated with a pulsing love that consumes your every thought?

Their plan was successful. With no criminal records and a passion to raise children in a stable and loving home, Grace and Matthew Edith finished their parent training and were quickly registered as a couple eligible to foster children. Within the year of finally deciding, the couple bought an old, three-story home. The house had six bedrooms, three full bathrooms, a basement, and a large backyard with a rock wall surrounding the property. It seemed as if it were the perfect house to raise children and make a difference.

The Edith couple would soon become foster parents—not for the money and benefits but to create a haven for struggling and abandoned children. Unfortunately, Grace could not conceive. Despite multiple efforts, the doctors could not find a solution and Matthew wasn't fond of the thought of using a surrogate mother to have children without

Grace. So, it made sense to foster and possibly adopt children to create the family they so desired.

That being said, Matthew wasn't entirely comfortable being a foster parent but he didn't like conflict and wasn't one to argue. And so, through constant persistence, he finally said yes. He loved Grace more than anything and hated the idea of making her unhappy.

The new Edith house was just on the edge of Effington. With no neighbors nearby and a lake within walking distance, this quiet and secluded spot seemed like the perfect place to raise Grace's dream family.

The house was more tall than wide, slightly narrow but with plenty of space. The enormous yard had an old swing set, a large oak tree, and a rock wall covered with thick green moss. Although some would say the house was too run-down and needed major renovations, Matthew knew it had strong bones and a lot of potential.

The couple purchased the house with all its contents at an amazing price. The only catch was that it had to be purchased in Bitcoin. Fortunately, they had plenty after Matthew acted on a tip from a friend, investing a lump sum of their savings. The couple found the price and payment option to be odd but were excited to have found such an incredible deal. Apparently, the seller had inherited his grandparent's home and needed to quickly pay off some gambling debt. Grace had been tirelessly browsing the internet for cheap homes matching her criteria and stumbled across the for-sale-by-owner.

The couple rushed the entire process but were still confident that it was worth it. Filled with love for each other, they believed it would guide them in their decisions toward this new chapter in life. Nothing could prevent their dedication and love for each other from thriving. Each respected the other's thoughts and celebrated their successes.

The way Grace smiled, revealing her dimples and the tiny wrinkles next to her eyes, mesmerized Matthew. He couldn't get enough of her;

from dusk until dawn, his mind was fixated on her. When Matthew laughed—like, *really* laughed—he would snort like a pig. Grace couldn't help but see the child in her husband and care for him more. Even with his broad shoulders and massive frame, she could see his tender heart. Together with this fervent love, they planned to raise children with the tender grace they believed they could offer.

The new spacious house felt empty, but the Edith couple knew that soon, it would be filled with underprivileged children who would thrive and call it home. Grace could barely contain her anticipation to finally be a mother and fulfill her greatest desire.

But instead of fostering their first child, family services proposed adoption and placed two children with them. The twins, Jonathan and Victoria, had tragically lost their parents in a house fire. As toddlers with no extended family, the Edith couple were granted custody during the placement process. They were not expecting adoption but had connected with the twins during the interview on a level they could not explain. From the moment they met, they felt as if the twins were their own.

During the first six months of raising Jonathan and Victoria, two more children were introduced to them for foster care. The young couple had proven their ability to provide a stable and responsible home life. With this new offer, Grace and Matthew began considering and taking the steps necessary to establish a group home. As the caretakers of the children, Grace and Matthew would receive more financial stipends from the state. They would be compensated for their help with a tally of daily expenses to use for the benefit of the foster children.

The new foster kids were significantly older than the adoptive children and they came with baggage, each carrying their own problems from their past experiences. Jayden and Patrick came from two separate backgrounds. The boys had similar upbringings, but their behavioral responses were quite different. Jayden was cautious and seemed self-absorbed, isolating himself from the family. He had come from a group home with more than sixteen kids, many of whom were troublemakers. Grace and Matthew had read through his file and certain indications revealed that the previous foster parents had neglected the children in their case.

At six and half years old, Jayden was one of the youngest, but often had to fend for himself. According to Jayden, he went hungry because there was not enough food. Sometimes, the foster parents would buy pizza and yell up the stairs, "First come, first serve." If Jayden wasn't down fast enough, then all the pizza would be gone with nothing else to eat. Matthew and Grace were eager to welcome him into their home where they vowed he'd never go hungry again.

Patrick, on the other hand, came from a situation where the foster parents were keeping the money and using it for themselves. When multiple complaints from the school were received because he had no school supplies or clothes, Patrick was removed from the family and transferred to the Edith's home.

Although shy, he was polite and good-natured. Patrick enjoyed helping with gardening, specifically the vegetables. Within his first few days of living in the Edith household, he built a beautiful garden box in the side yard all by himself. Although Patrick seemed to thrive during the day, at night, he had nightmares and would call out names in fluent Russian, tears flowing down his face. He refused to talk about his dreams when asked.

Patrick and Jayden were almost the same age. The twins were three years younger. Although challenging, Grace made it work and confidently handled the day-to-day. She established rules and strong morals to be the backbone of the Edith house. Grace and Matthew weren't really religious, but Grace relied on many proverbs from the Bible to teach their foster children life lessons. She loved decorations that had verses from the Bible on them. She often hung them in the bathrooms, bedrooms, and kitchen. She hung her favorite verse, Mark

12:31, "Love your neighbor as yourself," in the foyer so it was prominent when you entered their home.

Grace was raised Catholic while Matthew's upbringing was unconventional. His parents were hippies, and he grew up in a commune. The two married right out of high school. Matthew was good at math and established himself in an accounting firm in California. He built up plenty of savings and investments, so when Grace asked him to quit his job to move to Illinois, he knew it was possible. To support them, along with the financial stipends and their allocated savings, he became a truck driver. This gave him steady work and good pay, but he was away from the home for long periods of time and not always able to help with the day-to-day. Their financial status allowed them to buy top of the line appliances and provide generously for the children. He wasn't worried about the finances and Grace was literally glowing in her new role. Still, Matthew missed the accountant job. At least trucking was peaceful with no demanding clients and gave him time away from the energetic twins.

CHAPTER 1

The morning sunrise directed rays of light across Effington County. In unison with the sun, Grace and Matthew awoke and methodically started their daily routines. The sunlight poured in through the windows of the Edith home, illuminating the interior walls inch by inch. The house was quiet while the children were still asleep in their beds.

Today was a rare day. Usually, Grace would still be asleep while Matthew got ready. But today, the natural light reflected in her eyes, making her stretch and yawn. She made her way downstairs while he ate his egg whites with spinach, then kissed her goodbye. Squinting into the early sunlight, Matt stepped out the front door and chugged his black coffee like it was a shot. He then started up the ancient Volkswagen they'd found online and drove to his eighteen-wheeler. He was desperately looking forward to the second cup of coffee he'd grab at the gas station on the way. Grace, on the other hand, began her ritual coffee consumption, with milk and sugar lingering over the steam rising from her mug. She then took a leisurely shower and felt prepared for the start of her day just as Victoria barged into her room. She was a hot mess standing in the doorway in her pink pajamas, demanding breakfast. Grace quietly reminded her to whisper and not to wake the house. "Today is Saturday."

As Matthew arrived at his job, he parked and climbed up the driver's side of the tractor-trailer. Unlocking the door, he hopped in and leaned into the worn-down seat. With a grunt, he pulled the door shut, shook himself into a more comfortable position, and then finally took a sip of his second cup of steaming coffee. As the Colombian blend flowed down into his stomach, it filled his body with an inner warmth. Moving his calloused hands around the cup to absorb the heat, he took another sip and then pulled out his keys. Matt hung onto the truck's key after sifting through them all and let the rest fall down the keychain, clanging into each other. He inserted the key and turned it with a jiggle. At first, nothing. But then, with a second twist, the engine roared to life as thick, creamy black clouds poured out from the exhausts. Pulling out onto the road, Matthew was grateful for the late start. Today would be a short six-hour haul and he would still be home for dinner.

With her second cup of coffee, Grace swung open the large, heavy front door to their rural three-story house. Closing her eyes, she breathed in the fresh country air and listened to the birds twittering. Stepping outside onto the warm cement, she noticed a covered basket. Grace knelt and glanced around her, wondering how Matt had not noticed it on his way out. As she pulled back the thin blanket, she gasped and almost spilled her coffee. Her hand found its way to her heart as tears welled up in her eyes. A beautiful, dark-skinned baby with blue eyes stared back at her. At once, she brought the basket into the living room to examine the baby more closely. As Grace began to tend to the wet diaper, she remarked to herself, "Definitely a boy."

"I knew that," Victoria added in her baby voice. She had sneaked up and was peering over Grace's shoulder. "So, are we keeping him?" Victoria excitedly asked Grace.

"Why, of course. He was brought here for that exact reason. If I'm right, we'll have to follow up later."

"Yay, can I get the others?"

"Let them sleep. I don't think this child is going anywhere any time soon."

There was a moment of silence as she tried to secure the fresh disposable diaper that had been Victoria's and was much too large for the infant.

"Why is he staring at me?" asked Victoria.

"Right? He just keeps watching!" Grace replied, and then the two of them began chuckling together. The baby continued to quietly look at them, blinking his startling blue eyes every few seconds. Grace then swaddled him in the blanket.

"That's so much better, right?" she said to him and then told Victoria, "Throw this in the garbage for me, will you?"

"Uhh, okay. *Sniff, sniff.* How come baby poop doesn't smell?"

"Don't go smelling it, weirdo!"

Victoria giggled like a mad villain and ran off to throw it away. Grace laughed and turned back to the child. "She is strange, isn't she?"

Victoria sprinted back, filled with uncontainable energy. "But why?"

"I don't know, baby poop usually doesn't smell. I forget why "

"How come the baby had that cloth as a diaper?"

"I'm not sure. Maybe whoever dropped him here couldn't afford to buy diapers. They are very expensive," she added.

"That's sad."

"Yes, it is. But that's the exact reason why Matthew and I are here, right? To take care of you guys—our family!"

Victoria wrapped her arms around Grace's neck and responded, "I love you."

"Aww, I love you too, baby girl."

Victoria walked away smiling and went back to her room upstairs.

What shall we name you? Grace thought to herself. She grabbed the baby book of names on the shelf and began searching. As the day progressed, every child had an opportunity to interact with the baby.

John was annoyed for some reason; Jayden didn't seem to care, but Patrick was loving and attentive. He and Victoria spent most of the day playing with the baby. After most of the daily chores were finished, Grace finally settled on a name for the boy. She brought Victoria along with her to the back bedroom where there was a crib she put him in that they had never gotten around to dismantling.

"I've got a name for him now."

Victoria stood straight and peered in through the slats of the crib.

"Cinderella!" Grace announced.

"Really?" Victoria slightly turned her head in confusion. She attempted to force a smile but ultimately could not.

"Just kidding, silly goose."

They smiled at each other and then looked back at the baby. He seemed no older than ten months.

Earlier in the day, Grace finished checking with local authorities and the state's department of family and child services. There were no public birth records that seemed to match. In fact, it almost seemed as though the boy had appeared out of thin air. Child services granted temporary custody as they sorted out the next steps. Grace set up an appointment with the pediatrician and scheduled a blood test. Eventually, the foundling would become part of the Edith household as the search revealed no known family.

"Your name will be Isaiah because you will be our salvation," she said, slightly poking the baby on the nose. Isaiah smiled and slobbered, his first true demonstration of emotion. His bright blue eyes glistened in the sunlight, which reflected through the windowpane. Both eyes seemed like a vast ocean of color illuminated in his irises. As Grace examined his eyes closer to the center, she noticed they became a dark blue with subtle hints of brown. They were mesmerizing and glorious, as if universes were held together by the gravitational pull of his pupils.

Matthew had been home for a while. With a smile, he appeared at the door, dragging two little boys by his legs and carrying another on his shoulders. Grace smiled at Matthew and the boys and then turned back to the infant.

"Come look at this!"

"What, what is it?" Matthew asked. "Got a name?"

"Yes, actually. I think we should name him Isaiah."

"Good choice."

"But just look at his eyes," Grace added.

"Wow, that's really…peculiar, huh?" he commented, clearly unsure of what to say.

"Oh, just take a better look."

He leaned down and stared Isaiah's pupils intently in the eyes before standing up with a smile.

"Those—those are some pretty eyes. Isaiah is definitely a special boy. I'm glad they decided to let us keep him in our care for now. His adoption might be the easiest one yet." They both giggled and smiled wide.

"I know. It's almost too good to be true! This is destiny—it has to be."

Just last week, the foster care agency was proposing that they take on more kids and be a temporary group home for troubled and abandoned children. The agency encouraged their eagerness and desperately needed to place a long list of cases. The couple had agreed and were granted a higher rate for standard maintenance of the children. With four open spots, one was now filled. Isaiah moved quickly from foster child to adoption and became a permanent part of the household.

As the months passed, new placements were discussed, but it would be a few more years before additional children would join the household. Victoria and Patrick were the biggest help with Isaiah, and eventually, the new children that joined them, too. Victoria matured into a natural motherly role while Patrick was a gentle support, spending one-on-one time with them.

As Isaiah grew, he continued to express no emotion. The year was now 2010 and Isaiah was four years old. Benjamin, who was also four, had just joined the family. The moment they met, Isaiah stepped forward to greet him and a bond was formed. At times, you could hear Isaiah talking with Benjamin, even though he spoke to no one else. John ridiculed Isaiah and called him a mute.

The new foster child's full name was Benjamin Matthew McCoy. He was tiny and thin. He came from a family of five, with two sisters. He lost his entire family to a natural disaster.

As they hid in the basement of their home, the house lights flickered and the family cried in fear. His father commanded them all to recite prayers while a tornado ripped through the neighborhood. Ben watched in fear as his father begged God for mercy. Ben cried out to his father from across the room when the building collapsed on top of them. Miraculously, Benjamin, the youngest in the family, survived, protected by a flipped-over couch that somehow withstood the weight of the rubble. Ben was the only member of his family who did not join hands and pray. Instead, he took cover. Under wooden planks, insulation, and pipes lay the bloody mess of his family. When he saw the blood pooling on the floor, Ben broke down, rolling from side to side, crying and cursing God while firemen tried to comfort him and bring him to safety.

Eventually, paramedics, more fire department members, and the police arrived. They showered Benjamin McCoy with love, and he became property of the state. His father's house was the only one destroyed by the tornado. All the other houses in town were unscathed. Soon after the horrific event, he was placed with the Edith family. He felt nothing. All he could do was focus on the hate he had towards his father's god—his family's god—whom his father worshipped until he died. The thought of the God of gods, the Almighty One that his father preached about made Ben angry. How could he be the greatest god if he was the only one to live? If God exists, why would he let something so terrible happen? His father was a liar who did not protect them. Gods can't protect them because gods don't exist. This was all something a boy so young should not have to think about. In fact, it was something he didn't have to go through in the first place. He cursed the world, nature, people and even his own life. Isaiah listened to every outburst, every fit of rage, and every cry from Ben. Ben only told Isaiah what he saw that day, how he felt about it, and why God was not real. No one else ever heard something so personal from Benjamin. Isaiah was a great listener and would respond calmly with compassion. The only thing that Ben refused to listen to was Isaiah's belief in God and how it helped him with his own personal experiences.

CHAPTER 2

As time moved on, Ben learned to hide his anger and sadness. He buried his true thoughts and feelings, causing his heart to grow colder and leaving a sense of emptiness in its place. But Ben still struggled. At times, his anger would resurface, and he'd deal with it with his fists. His life and the raging emotions that he desperately tried to hide made him feel rotten. He was ashamed of his helplessness and did everything he could to hide it. Isaiah was the only one he could be real with, which is why they became inseparable.

The Edith household continued to grow, and now, with thirteen children, it was chaotic, even with the strict structure. "Treat your neighbor as yourself," was the motto of the house—and quite relevant—but each new child came with baggage and deplorable backgrounds.

Still, Grace was determined to give them a loving home and willingly accepted any placement she was assigned. She was a marvel but needed to enlist help from a live-in nanny. The nanny made it possible for Grace to continue supporting the thirteen children.

All the children in her care established some type of relationship with each other, although these relationships varied. Some were good and some were bad. Some were just flat out weird. At young ages, most of the boys acted like usual boys, nonsensical hooligans with an absurd amount of energy. Now, at seven years old, they had a pretty good grasp on this whole "life thing" and would totally be better than you at everything, or so Ben often yelled. The only calm one was Isaiah, who was scary, absurdly calm.

Grace had already dealt with her fair share of hooligans throughout the three years as a foster mother. She saw these little rascals as a challenge. The Edith house had thirteen children in total, with ten boys and three girls. They all ranged from four to twelve, with Jayden and Patrick as the eldest. Jayden was the oldest out of everyone and proudly assumed the responsibility that came with it. He grew into a wonderful role model for all the kids but wasn't very relatable or loving. The adopted twins, John and Victoria, were nine years old. They became extremely bossy and hypocritical. They followed their foster parents closely, making sure they brown-nosed their way through life, learning that doing so could get them where they wanted to go.

The youngest, at four years old, was Vinny, followed by Daisy, who was six. Daisy and Vinny were seemingly the nicest kids out of the bunch. Daisy, though young, was extremely outgoing and down to earth. Vinny was smart and well-rounded—a jack of all trades. They got along with everyone, even Ben and Isaiah, who rarely got along with the others, often causing fights and rebelling, not only to their siblings, but to their parents, as well.

Benjamin was the rebellious one. Isaiah simply followed his lead. It's not that Isaiah and Benjamin were bad kids, per se, but Benjamin, from a young age, was always reckless, impulsive, and erratic. He couldn't seem to keep his hands to himself, let alone stand still. He had trouble focusing and excelled at irritating others. Grace used to strap Ben down at night so everyone else could go to sleep in peace. The boy just wouldn't stop moving. Deep down, he was a kind-hearted kid; however, the way people treated him hurt his pride and stunted some of his mental growth. Any sense of self-control was completely lacking in all that he did.

Over time, his tendencies led him to being a bit of an outsider. The other kids didn't like him because he had ADHD and loved to start problems. And so, the separation from the group formed a wall in his heart. Ben thought that if he conformed to those around him and gave in to his foster parents, he would lose himself. Ben wanted to fit in and desperately wanted to be included. Yet, the last time he had a family, it was taken from him. He felt that if he grew too close to the foster kids and his foster parents, that he would experience the same loss again. His heart was eager to prove he did not need a family. Instead, he embraced his role as the outsider, assuming his position in the family as the token bad guy. As a result, Ben never really considered his foster family to be his real family. Except Isaiah, of course. He was like a brother to him. The epitome of a perfect child. He always listened, never talked back (unless he knew he was right), did his chores, sat still, and stayed quiet, unless Ben was pulling him around to indulge in shenanigans. The opposite of Ben, Isaiah was not very vocal or enthusiastic about anything. The other children didn't hate Isaiah at all. But Isaiah was just no fun, and he was always with Ben. No one understood the two, so they got along nicely.

There were also Alyssa and Jimmy, both five years old and probably the only normal kids of the bunch. These two did what they were told but were often led astray following their foster siblings, specifically Ben. As children, they followed their own simple motto, "Monkey see, monkey do." They were quite curious little kids with a decent moral compass but overall, they just wanted to be accepted.

Pablo was ten years old and different from the rest. He had a learning disability and was extremely introverted. He spent most of his time balled up with a book, refusing to play with others. The kids invited Pablo to participate in all the things they did. He never wanted to, but they kept on asking, day after day. Pablo was also bilingual, speaking fluent Spanish under his breath whenever someone pissed him off, which was apparently quite often. He seemed to be on the spectrum—just slightly. None of that bothered the other kids at first, but after a long time of asking and a long time of being cursed at in Spanish, they stopped interacting with him all together.

There was also Jack, who was six years old and just recently added to the Edith house. He seemed to be getting along with the others just fine, but the environment was very new to him and he was still adjusting to the house rules and mannerisms.

Lastly, the only other seven-year-old besides Ben and Isaiah was Shawn. Taken from his abusive parents just last year, he was still trying to fit in. He loved to play and watch cartoons; however, memories of his past constantly came boiling up, leaving him emotionally frustrated and often depressed. The other kids knew he was having an episode in which he was battling with the trauma of his past when his face would turn almost as red as his hair, highlighting the brown freckles on his face even more.

"Doing okay?" asked Grace as she sat down next to little Shawn. They were in the backyard, under the shade of the huge oak tree, sitting on a flowery white bench.

Shawn turned away from her and stared at the fence. She rolled her eyes and sat back.

"Fine. But I'm still gonna sit here."

"Go away."

"Nope."

"Yes."

"Never."

"Leave me alone!" Shawn yelled and ran across the yard, straight through the back door and all the way up to his room on the third level.

"Sheesh, he's a quick kid." Grace smiled.

"I'll get him," Matthew said, slowly following Shawn up the two flights of stairs.

"Leave me alone," Shawn repeated from under his covers.

Matthew smiled as he stood in the doorway. He walked into Shawn's room and stood beside his bunk bed. Shawn slept on the top bunk.

The third floor was where all the boys slept, taking up three bedrooms in total. Ben and Isaiah slept in the smallest bedroom but had their own beds. Their window looked out over the driveway. The two other rooms each had four kids. There were two bunk beds lined up against the wall in both rooms. These bedrooms overlooked the backyard. Every floor had a full bathroom, except the basement. Vinny, Jack, Jimmy, and Shawn all slept in one room, and Jayden, Patrick, John, and Pablo slept in the other. The second floor was where the girls along with Matthew and Grace slept. There was a room for the girls and the master suite for the foster parents. There were two small spare rooms downstairs on the ground floor for the occasional transfer, and so far, there have been no permanent takers—except for the nanny who took the first guest room.

"What's the matter?"

"Nothing. Get out of my room."

"Are you sure?"

"Yes!"

"Okay, fine. I was just gonna ask if you wanted to make some cookies with me."

Matthew began to turn away and walk out when he heard the covers move.

"Chocolate chip?"

Matthew returned to his side. "Well, obviously."

The room grew silent. Matthew thought about what else he could say to motivate him. "I really need someone to lick the spoon when I'm done, too. Can't let all that cookie batter go to waste."

Shawn shot up, throwing his covers off himself. With an eager smile and bright eyes, he said, "I'm the best at that!"

So, they made cookies. Baking was Shawn's favorite thing to do. It was the only time he couldn't contain his smile.

CHAPTER 3

As quickly as their home grew, so did the weight on Matthew's shoulders. Matthew wasn't handling the children every day and work really wasn't bad at all. The boulder on his back was due to the fact that his wife, whom he adored and loved so much, had no time for him. She was too tired and the intimacy between them began to fade as more important things than loving each other took over their lives. She had to deal with thirteen children in the house, although the young nanny was surely a huge help. He was busy working, and when he was home, he had little to no energy to contribute to the house and kids. He didn't know who got what in their lunch bag or who was allergic to what. He didn't know whose day it was to do the dishes. It upset him that he knew nothing of her world, and so, the stress began to weigh down on him, as he wondered whether that was contributing to the lack of intimacy between the two. And to top it all off, the only place he thought he could relax was filled with screaming and whining, mostly from ungrateful foster children. He could barely hear himself think. Over time, Matthew began treating them as just children, rather than his own. In his eyes, they weren't really his; he was just the husband of the wife who took care of them. All his fatherly duties began to dwindle, and the children rarely got to see his face, unless he was sitting in the living room staring at the TV.

Matthew was the only male adult, and he was unconsciously registered as a role model in many of the young imprinting minds of the children. A lazy, rebellious attitude grew in the house at an alarming rate, as if some horde of demons began to sway the minds of everyone who lived in the Edith house. Benjamin was most impacted by this, as the seven-year-old repeated Matt's cuss words and struck his foster siblings in acts of uncontrollable rage. Benjamin's constant state of anger infected the other children. Every time Matthew would leave for work and come back, the house would be more out of control, more violent, and more lawless.

The only coping mechanism that worked for him was alcohol, but Grace hated it. It was also prohibited in the house and dangerous with all the wandering, curious children around. So, Matthew would frequent bars and return drunk to sit down on his recliner and watch TV, ignoring his responsibilities completely. Matthew's character began to change; his thoughts turned against him. He couldn't stand to be in his own head or his own house. He hadn't kissed his wife in weeks. He knew they were drifting away from each other and felt as though there was nothing he could do.

Long hours on the road and the impending thought that he ruined his life by following Grace took an extreme toll on Matthew's mental health. Even with the radio playing and the windows down, without the love of his life, he couldn't escape his mind and the treacherous thoughts that invaded it. He had sips on the road, being cautious about how much he consumed so as not to attract any unwanted attention. The once vibrant and calming man grew lethargic and occasionally violent—nothing physical. He began to verbally abuse Grace with rude remarks and had an aggressive attitude towards her, likely from all the built-up hatred he had for the way their life had become.

None of it was acceptable in the least, but to Grace, things "could always be worse." Grace felt a deep bond with Matthew. So, it didn't matter how many lies he told or how many promises he broke. Grace kept calling him back to her. Matthew began to realize that Grace would never leave him, even when he wanted her to. He took advantage of her love and kindness and drank whenever he wanted. He promised to change, but never did. In fact, he never really planned to. Grace, however, grew trauma-bonded to Matthew. She couldn't leave him for the life of her. Matthew didn't want a wife that didn't have time for him, yet he didn't want to leave Grace to suppress his own insecurities. Matthew tortured her mind. She wasn't taking care of herself anymore. Her mornings grew gray. She rarely brushed her teeth, let alone brushed her hair or took a shower.

Instead of helping her up, getting down and dirty with his wife in the trenches of their scattered, fragile minds, he would just go back to try to get "some damn peace and quiet!" by saturating his liver and intoxicating his mind, fueling his evil thoughts with supreme quality gasoline. Drinking at the bar and sneaking canteens on the road was no longer enough for him. The noises in his head were too loud to ignore, so he needed to be drunk all the time to suppress them.

Matthew became more depressed and felt more vulnerable than ever before. To suppress his stress and hide his vulnerability, he chose to drink more, comfortably sitting with all the negative thoughts that plagued him. His heart turned to an icy stone, which had no room for love as his lack of compassion became his core. That was the beginning of the end. He would sneak bottles into his closet and drink when everyone was outside or sneak sips from canteens he hid in his coat. Her drank it all—beer, tequila, vodka, rum, and gin, you name it. Soon, the already unstable house came tumbling down, from whole to broken and finishing as shattered. The lives of these children were soon to be changed forever. Matthew and Grace did not realize what they had gotten themselves into.

CHAPTER 4

The lawlessness pursued by almost every child; each one was a troublemaker in one way or another. Especially Ben, John, and Alyssa. Grace couldn't keep up with all the school meetings and after school detentions. For one, John was selling gum on the school bus. He had conspired with Alyssa, and they were making serious cash. John was getting stockpiles of Juicy Fruit, Rainbow Stripes, Mentos Gum, Big Red, and Hubba Bubba. They had Orbit, Stride, Trident, Winterfresh, 5-gum, and even Big League Chew.

It was an organized elementary school robbery. He got the gum for dimes a piece and Alyssa helped him sell each pack for two dollars. Eventually, the school principal caught on and they had a long talk in her office. They were concerned this practice would progress into something else. Another school meeting was concerning Ben, who had brought a pocketknife to school and was showing other kids at lunch. He was suspended for two days, and Grace was reprimanded by the school for her supposed failures. Of course, the caretaker would be blamed for giving the children access to these materials and allowing the behavior to occur under her nose. These are elementary school kids, not high schoolers. Grace had defended herself and swore none of it was from her household—that it must be coming from the school and that it was happening under *their* noses. She still pledged "to scare those kids straight, with some motherly love." However, that was an empty promise.

Sure, she scared them, but it didn't quite work in her favor. Instead, it ended up making things worse. They were completely out of her control, and they had been for some time now. She blamed it on the moment she took in that sinister little boy, Ben McCoy. Grace no longer had that peppy and easy-going attitude. She was emotionally and physically drained, and she began to tune out the chaotic wilderness that surrounded her every moment of every day. She pretended as if the home she had built on firm morals and standards was still standing, when, in fact, it had imploded long ago. She swept the problems under the carpet to deal with them another day—or never at all. Why start something you don't have the energy to finish? Especially when behind on everything else like bills, budgeting, laundry, planning, meetings, appointments, punishments, and, of course, behind on dinner for the fourth night straight.

At eight o'clock in the evening, Grace pulled out two steaming hot trays of lasagna and then rang the dinner bell like a mad woman. What sounded like a thunderous stampede roared down the stairs as all thirteen kids spilled out into the main floor and into the dining room. The massive table fit all the children perfectly. She gave everyone one fat slice and stored the three leftover slices in the fridge.

"Momma, what about the game to see who gets seconds?" Alyssa asked with puppy eyes and an eager spirit.

"Only good girls and boys get seconds," she snarled back, then retreated into her study.

"I didn't even do anything," Jayden mumbled to himself.

"Grace has been acting real funky lately," added Ben.

"Ben, if you weren't such a delinquent, this wouldn't happen," accused Alyssa.

"Ha! You're one to talk, you two-faced bipolar bitch, damn snitch."

"John! I told you I didn't snitch!"

Then, the table erupted in anger and dispute. Food was thrown, drinks were spilled, and plates were broken. The kids had mouths like the truckers her husband worked with. Grace closed her eyes and pretended it wasn't even happening, ignoring it all and once again disconnecting herself from life and family. She leaned back in her chair and stared at the white ceiling of her study. She began to weep uncontrollably, her sadness transforming into anger and then fury. Grace stomped back into the room with eyes that resembled wild animals. John was closest to her and cursed first so she slapped him across the face.

The room went silent and then John began to cry and whine, "Why, Mom?"

The children were terrified, except Ben and Isaiah. Isaiah sat emotionless chewing on his lasagna. Ben smiled as John's face began to burn red. Grace slapped John again, then walked over to Ben and slapped him harder.

"Don't cry," she commanded. "If I hear any more foul language, get any more phone calls, or hear you kids fighting again, you will be punished severely. What John and Ben received were small warnings. Remember this and think about the consequences should you continue to disobey me. I am sick and tired of this animal house. This will stop. Today!"

All the kids nodded with eyes lasered to hers. They watched as she walked out of the room and went back to her study. The kids finished dinner, did the dishes and all their evening chores quietly. All of them went to sleep without uttering another word. Two days passed and the children all stayed relatively silent. Of course, they talked at school but not at home.

Ben was determined to get John into more trouble. Ben hated John and didn't even know why. Overall, he was an average kid; other kids did far more annoying things but for some reason, all of Ben's anger was focused on John. His squinty eyes, his pasty skin, his high-pitched voice, his constant complaining, and his snake-like tendencies infuriated him. All that John was, Ben hated. He didn't see anything good in him.

"Hey, Victoria?" Ben asked, sneaking into her room after the children were sent to bed. Grace was downstairs drinking wine with the nanny and Matthew was in deep sleep on the couch.

"What? I'm trying to sleep." She left her pink night mask on.

"John stole your money. I saw him take it."

"What!" Victoria ripped off her mask and shot up. She looked under her bed and pulled a small wooden bat out. Ben smiled. "I'm going to hurt him."

She paced into John's room and without hesitation, she brought the bat to his head while he laid in his bed. John immediately woke up in pain, screaming, crying, and holding his head. Suddenly, Victoria's stomach turned. She jumped back and put her hands in front of her mouth. "I'm-I'm sorry. I didn't think it would hurt that much."

John didn't answer; he was still rolling in agony and his head began to swell up.

"I'm sorry! Please stop screaming. I'm sorry," she pleaded.

"What the hell happened?" Grace appeared at the entrance to the boys' room. "Why are you here? You hit him? Why did you hit him?"

Victoria looked towards her influencer, Ben, who was nowhere to be found.

"I-I-He stole my money! My piggy bank money!"

"No, I didn't," John cried out.

Grace slapped Victoria across the face. She began to tear up and with one sniffle, her nose began to drip blood.

"Don't hit people! Especially with bats."

John and Victoria were both crying, and the rest of the house was wide awake now, listening in their bedrooms.

"John, did you take her money?"

"No, I swear." He was still groaning.

"What makes you think he did this?"

"Ben told me," she cried.

Grace's face contorted as if she were lifting a car. Her veins popped and her jaw clenched.

"Apologize to John and get him ice. We'll discuss your punishment tomorrow."

Grace's adrenaline was through the roof. Obviously, Ben was behind it all, who else?

"Oh shit," Ben said as he heard Grace coming to the room. Isaiah was sound asleep; drama never interested him. Grace ripped Ben off his bed and grabbed his ear, leading him downstairs. All the kids were out of their beds watching from their doors as Ben begged for mercy. They got downstairs and Grace grabbed a metal spatula from a kitchen drawer. She pulled up his shirt and struck him three times, leaving a bruised back. Ben didn't cry but he yelled in pain when he was struck. Eyes wide open and tapping her feet uncontrollably, she pushed Ben to the floor. He was laying on his stomach on the kitchen floor with his shirt pulled up. She began striking him again, and again, and again. When he started to bleed, she paused for a moment, Ben was breathing heavily and mumbling under his breath.

"Still gonna talk back?"

Grace started hitting him again, with more power in each blow. Ben began to cry.

"Finally, that's all we needed. For you to learn your lesson."

She dropped the spatula into the sink and nudged Ben onto his side with her foot. He was silent with watery eyes and his head down. All he felt was shame and the need for revenge. To kill his foster mother with his own two hands. All he could imagine was strangling her until she went blue and lifeless. He wanted to scream at her and tell her how wrong she was. Yet, he bit his tongue realizing his place in that moment.

"The hell is wrong with you? You better change, fast."

Ben nodded. The kids ran back to their beds as they heard him slowly ascend the stairs. Climbing back into bed, he cried and sniffed himself to sleep while Isaiah slept like a rock, unbothered, arms and legs folded like a pretzel and drool leaking on his pillow.

CHAPTER 5

It seemed like Matthew and Grace were doing better. Their wave of heartache seemed to fade away just as fast as their love rekindled itself. Matthew suddenly stopped drinking at home and on the road. He still frequented the bars, but he was generally happier. Happy that he had his wife back again. He never wanted to lose her love and knew that he would break through heaven's gates just to get her back. Or so he told her. He called Grace his angel and held her as divine. He talked to her with love and kindness once again, and Grace fell even more madly and passionately in love with him. However, even with their refurbished relationship, their life demanded their time and effort now more than ever and that's something they both understood. With Matthew actually helping a little more, Grace had more energy, and they had more time to be intimate with one another.

But their relationship was still different. Matthew had—at his core—become a narcissistic psychopath, and Grace a borderline psychopath. Yet they basked in the glory of their toxic love, convincing themselves that nothing had changed between them.

"We took on too many kids. One rotten apple ruined them all and they are out of control," Grace said while talking to Matthew in bed one day.

"Look, I can start working weekends only, if my boss will allow it. We have the money, especially with our savings and the benefits that flow in. It won't be a big deal if I stop working for a couple of months."

"Stop working?"

"No, no. Just work less so I can help out more around the house."

"It's odd of you to be recommending such a thing."

"Yeah, well, I'm sick of driving and clearly you could use more of me. They need a father figure, and some more discipline."

"I agree. Could you start by making breakfast tomorrow?"

"Ugh," he joked with an eye roll. "I mean, of course." He smiled and then they fell asleep in each other's arms. During the night, Grace rolled away from his warmth, preferring to lay on her own.

The entire Edith household was filled with the aroma of bacon and eggs that following morning. The children awoke with a smile on their faces for the first time in a long time.

"Good morning, rascal," Matthew said, handing Ben a plate toppling with eggs.

"Morning," he groaned back, rubbing his eyes. He happily accepted the breakfast, trying his hardest to hold back a smile, but still, a slight grin found its way out.

"Hey, Matthew, thanks for breakfast!" screamed Victoria. She was always far too loud in the morning. She patiently waited for a plate and then brought it with her to the large table.

"Sure thing."

Victoria pulled her chair out, placed her food on the table, and sat down. "Oops, I forgot juice! Want some juice, too?" she asked Ben innocently.

"Um, sure."

"What's the magic word?"

"Please?"

She smiled and returned with two plastic cups filled with orange juice.

"Thanks."

"You're very welcome," she said as she dug into her plate of eggs.

Victoria loved to be of service. She loved to help. But she also loved justice and she had just handed Ben a tall glass of revenge that he devoured alongside his bacon and eggs.

Matthew watched as the children ate. It was quiet. Suddenly, Matthew realized that he really was the foster father of thirteen children. He must have counted all the children four separate times before succumbing to his rising anxiety and feeling extremely overwhelmed. Although he wonderfully managed breakfast, he was still worried.

The nanny helped all the kids get prepared for school and walked them out to their bus stop just down the street. They arrived at the stop just seconds before the bus pulled up next to them. The nanny sent them off and the bus driver gave her a horrid wink.

Ben, however, was left behind, sitting in the bathroom, glued to the toilet, releasing all that was inside his stomach. He was dressed, had his teeth brushed, and his bag all packed. However, he couldn't manage to make it out of the bathroom, thanks to his malfunctioning bowels.

Grace had finally made it down the stairs, entirely trusting that Matthew would handle their morning shift, which he did. She had a frizzy head of hair that looked like a bird's nest. Matthew had made more breakfast for just the two of them and even whipped something up for the nanny, too. The three of them ate in the dining room, breathing a sigh of relaxation and relief, only to hear Ben groaning upstairs. The adults dropped their heads down and sighed again. This time was going to be the last time Ben would ever get caught missing the bus. They were fed up.

Ben was still on the toilet, hunched over in pain, with no idea as to why this was happening. His head snapped towards the bathroom door when he heard the nanny jiggling the handle.

"Unlock the door, Benjamin," the nanny said.

"No, I'm using it right now," he mumbled.

"You missed the bus. You know you're in trouble when you get out," she warned and walked back downstairs. "He said he's still using it," the nanny mentioned as she approached the foster parents.

"Great, this'll take a while." Matthew sat down and ate his food.

"What are you sitting down for?" Grace barked.

"What do you mean? Kid's clearly sick or something."

"I don't care. Fine. I'll do it."

Grace opened the kitchen drawer and grabbed the wooden spatula. She stomped away towards the stairs. Matthew kept eating his food, unbothered. The nanny watched the situation with utter abandon.

Ben's stomach still felt terrible, but he decided to flush the toilet and prepare for his doom. He stared at himself in the mirror as he washed his hands, wondering why he was even alive. This was no life to live.

As Ben opened the door, he saw Grace coming up the stairs. Accepting his fate, he walked up to her. Without a word, she grabbed his wrist and pulled him in front of her. She lifted his shirt and began beating Ben. After about five or six strikes, she pushed Ben away from her.

"Why do you keep doing this? Huh? We give you everything you need yet you trample on our generosity. Get in the car; the nanny will drive you to school."

Ben said nothing and did as Grace commanded. The nanny drove Ben to school, lecturing him all the way. Ben stared out of the window and watched as the trees passed by, completely ignoring her.

Ben never missed the bus again, though as time passed, his antics at school grew worse. Throughout the year, he was constantly getting into trouble. School was always rough for the foster kids. Most of them were called losers or loners, according to the rest of the small elementary school elite, who all loved to pick on others. Victoria and John, however, were considered cool or normal because they had been adopted by the Edith family and weren't just some foster kids like the rest of them. Everyone knew John and Victoria, and that helped with their introduction into middle school.

The foolishness of elementary school would only increase to madness in middle school. There were more hangouts, more problems, and more trouble. Even with a nanny and two full-time parents, there were still many kids to keep track of and too many personalities in the house just waiting to clash. Matthew was home most of the time. It seemed he wasn't a day drinker anymore and helped out as much as he could, but it was still a lot. At night, Matthew would indulge in a drink here and there. But on some nights when Grace was out or already asleep, he would get blackout drunk and wake up without a clue as to what he did the night before. These nights the children were left to deal with his midnight stumbles or rude and off-putting comments.

Early in the school year, there was a fall festival that happened in town. The kids went pumpkin picking and apple picking, went on hayrides, and travelled through the corn maze.

Children ran all over while Matthew and Grace sat down at the bench sipping on some hard cider that warmed their bodies. The steam rising from the fresh cider fogged up Matthew's sunglasses. It was very sunny out but quite chilly, as well.

Matthew lowered his sunglasses and looked Grace in the eye. "I love you."

"That's random."

Matt pushed his sunglasses back on, taken aback. "What do you mean?"

"You haven't been very loving lately," Grace snapped out of nowhere.

"Why do you say that? W-What do you mean?" he stuttered, confused.

She scoffed, "I mean that you haven't been here for me."

"What are you talking about? I stopped going to my job just to stay with you more," Matthew whined, thinking he had rekindled the relationship.

"Yeah, you did." She looked away from him.

"So, how am I not here?" he beckoned.

"You're drunk. Every day, you're sneaking a drink or sneaking to the bars. And you act like no one notices. Everyone notices. Thankfully, the children that know don't care enough to spread the news."

"I-I am not! I haven't even been to the bars," he stammered.

"Sure, keep lying to yourself. Ya dick!"

"I'm a dick? Really? I found your bottle of beer in the trash a while ago. I know you've been drinking, too." They lowered their voices, realizing the public setting.

"What are you talking about? I don't even like beer. Now you're making up shitty lies to excuse yourself."

"I swear."

"When was this, Matthew?"

"I-I don't know. Like a month or something."

She scoffed again. "You disgust me. How can you keep doing this to me?"

"Gracie, I'm not lying."

"Don't call me that."

"But…" he went silent. "Fine, have it your way." He stormed off knocking the hot cider over.

Grace sat there for a moment, calmly walked to the restroom, and then began to cry. The nanny found her and comforted her. She helped her compose herself. The two returned to care for the children.

Benjamin and Isaiah strolled through the fall festival as dry autumn leaves crunched under their feet and the aroma of hay, cinnamon, and pumpkin spice filled the air. Benjamin took a long, deep breath just admiring the different colors of the season. He moved his eyes like a newborn baby, looking through the night like a hawk until a particular treat caught his attention

"Yo, Isaiah," Ben said, grabbing his shoulder.

"'Sup?"

"Look how good those look."

"Yeah, I love apple cider donuts. Covered in brown sugar, still hot from baking. Muah! Just beautiful."

"Alright, weirdo. So, you like them. I get it." Ben continued. "Let's take 'em."

"Why?"

"Well, don't you want them?"

"Yeah."

"We have no money."

"Exactly. That's why we're going to take them. Look, no one is watching. Let's just grab a few real quick."

"I don't know, man."

"C'mon, quick. Just watch for me. I'm gonna jump over the counter and grab them."

"You're crazy, Ben."

"It's not like they need the money. We need the food more."

"They're donuts… we aren't dying of starvation," Isaiah shot back at Ben's logic.

Ben ignored his comment and jumped over the counter. Isaiah began to survey the area for any eyes. "Hurry up, man," he urged.

"I am, hold on. Oh, look! A bag. I got a bag."

"Hurry up!" Isaiah said as people started to appear, a few even beginning to look over. "We gotta go."

"Let's go!" Ben said, jumping back over the counter.

"Look! They're stealing!" a woman yelled.

A white lady with her pumpkin spiced latté spotted them and alerted the staff members. She even pointed the boys out. They were on a bench eating from the heavy brown bag of sugared cider donuts.

"See," Isaiah said, taking a bite. "I told you not to do it."

"Shut up!"

They ran away but the staff member was young and surprisingly fast. Still, no one caught up to Ben and Isaiah. They lost him as they turned a corner, using the moving hayride to their advantage. Then, they dipped into the corn maze and ran until they knew for sure no one would catch them, let alone find them.

They slowed their pace to a calm and steady walk as they took their time eating the donuts Ben had snatched. As they continued through the maze, they arrived at its heart to find Alyssa and Daisy. The two were sitting down in the middle of the path, probably assuming no one would pass by, especially this late; no one usually uses the corn maze after four in the afternoon. The girls were crying, mainly Alyssa though. Daisy was tearing up, but it was clear Alyssa was in pain.

"What's wrong?" Isaiah asked. He rushed to her side as soon as he had seen her, leaving Ben behind. Ben followed, taking his time as he munched on another donut.

"A lot," Daisy responded for her.

"Toughen up," Ben said, digging into the brown paper bag for another scrumptious treat. Isaiah turned. He was clearly aggravated. He punched Ben in the arm, shifting his balance.

"Ow." Ben rubbed his arm.

"You toughen up." Then, he turned back to Alyssa and knelt beside her. "What's wrong?" he asked again.

Alyssa sniffled. "It's about Matthew."

"What about me?" asked Ben.

"She said Matthew, not you! Selfish prick," Daisy remarked.

"Damn. Okay, my bad." Ben motioned himself away.

"What did he do?" Isaiah leaned in closer, kneeling beside her. He put his arm around her shoulder. Daisy was happy to see Isaiah giving her support and clearly noticed the passion he had for her.

"He tried to touch me."

"What? When? Where?" Isaiah looked furious.

"Last night. He came in and watched me. He just stood at the door frame while I did my hair. He was clearly drunk. Slurring his words, he said, 'You look pretty.' I don't even think he could stand without leaning on the wall. He stumbled towards me and looked at me in the mirror while I finished my braid. He touched my shoulder and slowly squeezed. I felt him gawking at me. He even licked his lips. I got up and left as fast as I could. He came downstairs and I told him that made me uncomfortable. His drunk ass didn't even remember being in my room. He barely even knew who I was."

Isaiah was listening intently the whole time as she vented and told him how inappropriate Matthew had been when he got blackout drunk, which was often now.

"That's terrible," Isaiah commented.

Daisy spat on the ground. "He's worse than you even know."

Neither the nanny nor Grace knew. They left him alone with the kids all the time. Too often, he gave up on his responsibilities, drowned himself in alcohol, and paid no attention to anyone in that house.

After what Ben and Isaiah heard, they never looked at Matthew the same. Isaiah wasn't confrontational but when he did butt heads with the foster father, he gave him a piece of his mind—in the most respectful manner of course.

After learning about how their foster father was behaving, the boys convinced the girls to tell Grace and the nanny. After hearing the reports from the girls, Grace was furious, but not with Matthew. "How could you say that?" Grace didn't believe one word, or better yet, she didn't *want* to believe a word. Instead, she punished the girls and ended the conversation there.

Ben and Isaiah no longer looked at their parents the same. Their foster parents were as evil as the bullies at school and the criminals on television. So, after seeing all that had transpired, Ben thought to himself, *Why try to act good when even good people are bad?*

He decided that being good meant being fake. Ben hated being fake more than anything else in the world. And so, Ben himself became the evil he hated, the bully, the criminal, and the instigator. Now that young Ben was growing older, he began to notice the changes in himself and the changes in all his friends and foster siblings, especially Isaiah, who seemed to hit puberty earlier than everyone else. Isaiah was a physical and mental masterpiece; he had a sculpted body that looked as strong as a horse with a mature mind that made decisions with speed and accuracy. The more time passed, the more obvious it became that Isaiah was a prodigy, meant for something far greater than being just another orphaned boy in the foster system. He had straight *A*s and he outperformed everyone in sports, standing at five foot seven and weighing in at one hundred and sixty pounds. It was clear that Isaiah would go on to be a sports star, a scientist, or maybe even the next president. Isaiah's growing prestige seemed to outshine everyone and

J.K Anderson

therefore put everyone around him in his shadow. Ben was becoming insecure and anxious that he would be left behind and abandoned by the only person that ever actually cared for him.

39

CHAPTER 6

"Yo, Zay," Ben called to Isaiah during their lunch period.

"Yo," Isaiah responded with little emotion.

"Umm, like. I'm just confused." He sat down next to Isaiah with a bag of chips in his hand.

"What's up?" Isaiah reached his hand into the chip bag and snacked with Ben.

"Why? Like, why are you so…um…"

"Spit it out, Ben." Isaiah became serious with a stern voice as he crunched the chips.

"Bro, how are you so big?"

"Oh." Isaiah was relaxed again. He swallowed his mouthful of crunched chips and answered, "I don't know, genetics I guess."

"Yeah, but like… It's gotta be more than that."

"I work out every once in a while."

"When? You're always with me." Ben was annoyed at the answer, as if Isaiah were lying.

"Ben, we aren't together every minute of every day."

"True. So, what do you do when you work out?" he asked suspiciously.

"I mean, I do push-ups, pull-ups, sit-ups, planks, and jump squats."

"Damn, a lot of ups. That's actually more than I expected. Now it makes sense."

"Sure, I guess so."

The bell rang and sent them off to their next class.

From that day on, Ben began mimicking Isaiah's workout routine every day, even when he was sore and even when he didn't feel like it. Week by week and month by month, Ben grew stronger and stronger. He watched his body with pride as it grew in the mirror before him. The more that his physique grew, the more that his confidence grew, too. Isaiah took notice of the transformation. He said nothing except the occasional, "Keep it up," for motivation. At the same time, Isaiah grew stronger and smarter.

While Ben was a bully, it was known around school that he wasn't one to pick on those weaker than him. He only bullied the bullies and the kids older and stronger than he was. This didn't always work out for Ben. In fact, these situations often flipped on him, as he became the one being bullied. Most people did not like Ben but it was clear to those that knew him that Ben was struggling with something inside himself.

"You good?" Isaiah asked during their lunch period together.

"Yeah yeah, I'm good." Ben seemed tired and annoyed.

"You sure? You got a black eye again."

Ben hid his face with his hood. "Yes, damn! Leave me alone!" He stormed out of the lunchroom and sat outside, alone and away from everyone.

Isaiah stayed at the lunch table, leaving Ben alone. He quietly ate his ham and mayo sandwich. Isaiah finished his meal and went to his next class before the bell rang. He stood at the door when the second bell rang, waiting for all the students to leave before entering. Then, Isaiah walked in and sat down near the middle section. Alyssa walked in moments after with a smile. She skipped over to his seat and placed her books down softly on the desk next to his. She sat down beside him, and the class began to fill up. Soon, the lesson would be in session. This was the only class Isaiah and Alyssa shared together. And so, they always made sure to sit side by side. In fact, they had been growing closer with every conversation ever since the corn maze back in the fall. It was spring now and school was almost over. They couldn't wait for the summer, but something else was on Isaiah's mind.

"Hey!" Alyssa nudged into Isaiah as she settled in her seat.

"Hi," he responded in almost a whisper.

"What's up? You look bummed."

"I'm just worried about Ben."

"Yeah, me too. He's starting to remind me of our foster father."

"What do you mean?" Isaiah shot up in his seat.

"Not that way." Isaiah eased back. "Look, as Matthew started being around after quitting his job or whatever, Ben got more depressed, like Matthew was the cause of it all."

"How?"

"I don't know. Maybe it's because Matthew can be so mean and harsh. He's so blunt and strict and ugh, I hate him. Anyways, Ben is repeating all the bad things Matthew says. He's hating on people because people are hating on him. He curses like it's his job, as if he were some rapper or something."

Isaiah nodded his head and listened.

"He needs to get a grip, honestly! Matthew is too far gone, but Ben. Ben can change."

"Settle down over there!" the teacher remarked. They were growing loud.

Alyssa continued with a soft tone, "He's losing his friends, his mind, and his grades. Although his grades have never been that good." She continued, "I'm worried, too. You should talk to him."

"I've tried. He doesn't want to talk to me."

They paused and looked ahead, paying attention to the teacher and her lesson. Isaiah sighed and leaned back, slouching to the right side of his chair. Alyssa nudged him slightly and leaned in, "Hey, he will listen to you. You're the only one he ever listens to."

The class continued and the two stayed quiet for the rest of the lesson. The school day came to an end, and all the students got on their respective bus headed home.

On bus 332, the last stop of the day was where eighty percent of the kids got off. The big yellow bus came to a screeching halt and its red stop sign extended from the side, flashing. The entirety of the students left on the bus flowed out from the folding doors as soon as they opened. Daisy, Vinny, Jimmy, Jack, Alyssa, Pat, Pablo, Shawn, Ben, Victoria, John, Jayden, and Isaiah poured out one by one. The group of thirteen were all going down the same dirt road, to the same driveway, which led to the same big house.

Ben walked in the middle of the road just to show how much of a badass he was. Isaiah followed closely behind, entertaining Ben's thoughts and keeping him calm.

Daisy, Victoria, and Alyssa walked together off to the right side of the road on the grass. Each girl was a different age, different height, and came from a different background, but they still got along for the most part.

Patrick, Pablo, and Vinny walked on the other side of the road, safely off the pavement, as well. They didn't really talk; they just watched while Vinny trailed ahead kicking stones as he went.

Shawn, John, and Jack walked about ten yards behind them talking about the sports news they had heard earlier in the day. The daring trades, unfortunate injuries, miserable losses, and surprising wins.

Further ahead of everyone, leading the group, was the eldest, Jayden. He didn't care for company and always walked alone.

Today, Victoria felt like he needed a friend and wanted to be nice, or at least appear nice to everyone else.

"Wait up!" called out Victoria.

"Why?" he responded.

Victoria looked puzzled, "Because…"

"I'm going to leave this dump in a couple of years. I don't want to be bothered in the meantime." Jayden pressed forward, not turning to address Victoria formally.

"Oh, okay then." Victoria rolled her eyes and turned to Alyssa.

"What an asshole." Alyssa said, trying to validate Victoria's reaction.

"I know, right? Like what did I even do?"

"He's a jerk. Forget about him."

The group proceeded to the large house and continued up the stairs to their designated bedrooms. Matthew was at work; he was called in at the last minute to cover someone who had fallen ill. Grace was out shopping for groceries and the house nanny stayed home cleaning the ground floor.

Benjamin and Isaiah were the last to enter the house. They loved to take their time. As they were shutting the heavy wooden door behind them, they looked out and saw a man stumbling down the street, mumbling about something incomprehensible. They shut the door and went to their room like the rest of the kids. The day continued with the kids finishing their homework and doing their chores. Matthew arrived home at around six. He said nothing to anyone; instead, he took a nap.

"Look," pointed out Victoria.

The girls huddled around and stood above Matt as he slept on the couch, drooling into the fabric.

"A shame," said Daisy.

"Why does Matthew drink so much?" asked Alyssa.

"Cause Grace is a bitch and Matthew's a bum," Daisy explained.

"Grace is amazing; don't ridicule her!" Victoria added with some sass.

"Ah, you're just a brown noser. Stop kissing her ass."

"How about I kick your ass instead?" Victoria squeaked, afraid of the words that had just left her mouth. She cowered back a step.

"Oh? You wanna fight me? Ha!" Daisy stood proud.

"No, I just—"

"Ugh!" Disgusted with Matthew and annoyed with Grace, Daisy paced away before getting infuriated with Victoria.

The next night, Matthew came home drunk again, falling into the walls as he made his way up the stairs. All the kids were awake in their beds and they all quietly listened to their foster father try to make it to his bedroom. The night ended with a bitter taste in everyone's mouth, especially Grace, who was awoken by her drunk husband asking for intimacy. She declined, as she always did when he was drunk, which was nearly every day and every night at this point. She rolled over and tried to get some sleep. Grace felt a hole eroding inside her, eating her soul from the inside out.

"Good morning," Matthew said with a smile.

"Ugh," Grace responded, rolling out of bed and standing at her night stand. She stared at the floor almost thoughtless. She then turned and peered into his eyes with the same look, "Are you serious?"

"What? What is it?" Matthew's squinted eyes were wide open now.

"I can still smell it on your breath. Go back to the couch. Why did you sleep with me?"

Grace left him before he could answer and went to brush her teeth. Matthew laid back down on the bed and let out a deep sigh. He slowly dragged his hands down his face and groaned in frustration. Matthew got up, made breakfast, and sent the thirteen children on their way to school. The nanny was giving each child lunch in a brown bag as they left. One by one, she would stop them at the door, drop the lunch in their school bag, and zip it up.

"Capri-sun?" little Vinny asked.

"Yes, yes. Now go. You'll be late."

"Yus!" Vinny fist pumped the air with victory written on his face.

She shuffled him out the door and moved to the next one like an assembly line.

"You did peanut butter this time?"

"Yes, I changed it, just like you asked," the nanny reassured her as the child was reluctantly pushed out the door and pointed to the bus stop.

"But still with the jelly right?"

"Yes, Alyssa, just as I said. Now go!" The nanny laughed as she shut the door. Matthew watched as the nanny scooted the last remaining child out of the door and smiled. He turned away and walked to the screen door, which led to the backyard. That's where Grace was, in her favorite seat with her feet on the chair and her knees up. She held a cup of steaming black coffee and listened to the birds sing their songs.

"What's wrong?" Matthew interrupted the chirping birds. Grace ignored him and took a sip of her coffee. "C'mon, Gracie."

"No, you know. I've had enough of it. You drink to wake up. You drink to go to sleep. You drink to work. You drink to relax. All you do is drink!" she yelled, almost spilling her coffee. The nanny heard them arguing, shook her head, and went upstairs to make sure the children made their beds.

"Gracie…"

"Don't call me that. Man up or get out. How can I raise this family with a drunk? Even with the nanny's help it is still overwhelming.

Yeah, you make breakfast and help out here and there, but you don't help me. We haven't made love in over a year."

"That's not my fault, I—"

Before he could finish, Grace interrupted him, "I don't know who you are anymore! Frankly, it *is* your fault. It's all your fault."

"I didn't realize I was letting you down so much."

"Well, you are."

There was a moment of silence. Matthew began to speak but stopped himself. He stuttered a word but then kept it to himself. "Okay. I'll man up. I'll do better."

"You're gonna have to." She didn't once look him in the eyes, keeping her own eyes glued ahead to the trees. "You always say that but it's just a cycle of pain. I'm sick of it."

"I am serious this time. Let me break the cycle. I'm sick of the way we are living, too. We will get better. I know it."

"You always know, huh?"

It was silent. Matt wanted to say something else, but he could think of nothing. Grace felt worse now, even though he wasn't fighting back, and even though she had called him out. Each time they talked, it was like a heavyweight battle of willpower and who will come out correct. Grace still felt like she had lost the conversation. She felt empty, and nothing could fill the void that had consumed her completely, growing bigger and bigger with every passing day.

Mathew walked back inside, destroyed. Grace stayed outside, defeated. They both knew they were losing control and had lost the love they once had.

I need a drink, they both thought to themselves.

Matthew started cleaning up the kitchen, wiping the counters with a foggy mind, and putting away the dishes. However, all he could think about while stuck in the trance was how he was letting his family down.

It ate at his pride and fueled his anger. Grace was still sitting outside staring across their fenced backyard, still looking at the same spot she was when Matthew was talking with her. The branches swayed in the wind and their green leaves shimmered under the sun.

It had already been eight years here in Illinois, the prairie state. The paths around the yards were marked by trails of dirt, which had been pounded in continuously by the children's play. There were patches of vibrant green and lines of dirt where grass was forbidden to grow. The swing set to the left was old and the wood was peeling. The earth underneath had divots where the children would kick off from. So much time and effort had been put into these kids. Grace felt as if her gift of motherhood was being abused and disregarded. She felt abandoned by everyone she loved.

At least I have my Victoria, but she's a little brown nose. I can't tell if she loves me. Grace could not lean on her alcoholic husband; she had left her friends in California and burnt many bridges. She had no family left who shared her blood and she couldn't continue her line. Her family name would die with her, and all her stories would be lost in the wind. *What's the purpose of all this, anyway?*

Matthew did better, just as he had promised. He was always on breakfast duty and made sure his wife and the nanny had a full belly before he did. He learned how to run eight errands in one day and still have the energy to deal with thirteen children. Matthew fixed things all around the house. He cleaned the gutters and fixed the roof. He stopped the upstairs leak and the downstairs faucets. He took out the garbage and cleaned the bathrooms. He did so much that Grace had trouble finding chores to give the kids. He even offered to help the kids with their homework—well, the kids that would let him. Jayden didn't care for any of his foster parents' help. He did his own homework, his own laundry, his own dishes, his own taxes, his own savings, his own cooking. and even paid his own phone bill. He was the only kid in the entire house who had a phone. Phones were actually prohibited among the children in the Edith house. However, Jayden bought it without permission with his own money that he had worked for. He paid all the expenses and continued to pay all its bills. Jayden worked two jobs as a waiter and a mechanic and had plenty of money to spend.

Benjamin didn't do his homework. He would wait until the morning of and then scramble to get it done the period before or cheat off Isaiah. Isaiah was a genius prodigy who excelled at everything and anything that he put his mind to. Everyone envied him but no one wanted to be his friend. He was just too boring for all the other kids; he was like a robot. He was too mundane, too disciplined, and too much of a goody two shoes. Isaiah didn't care for much at all; he did his chores and was respectful, but he didn't go out of his way for anyone. Except Benjamin. Ben was different. Ben had Isaiah in the palm of his hand without even realizing it. They were as close as brothers, as thick as thieves.

All the other kids let their foster father help them with things like homework, although most did it reluctantly. He wasn't a bad help though. He actually wanted the children to learn the material and spent the time needed to make sure they got it and understood before moving on, rather than doing it for them or simply getting the answer and not reviewing. Matthew was not the best father, but he was trying hard, especially in the last few months after what Grace had told him.

One afternoon, while the children were all out at school and the nanny was out getting groceries, Matthew saw an opportunity for some alone time with his wife. He made sure he smelled good and brushed his teeth for good measure. He had been on a roll the past month or so. Matt was actually proud of himself for once. He loved his wife again and didn't need alcohol as the center of his life. He needed Grace. She made life easier to live when they got along. Matthew tiptoed up to their bedroom where he presumed his wife was, either reading a book or taking a nap. He slowly opened the door and saw his wife had just finished a shot of tequila. She tried to hide it but fumbled the empty glass onto the carpet floor. Her eyes left the glass and slowly looked up at Matthew. He squinted his eyes and raised his eyebrows, looking for the words to speak. Matthew raised his hand to his mouth in disbelief, eyes fixated on his helpless wife. He seemed calm yet fierce, cold and distant. Matthew turned away and walked downstairs without uttering a word.

The house was already hanging by a thread. The backbone had been shattered and all that was left was the poor nanny. Matthew resumed his drinking, and the nanny was, of course, not clueless to all that was transpiring in the Edith household. She was young, however, and being paid more than what she was worth. So, she kept her mouth shut and her eyes forward. Most of the children followed suit. The cheerful, vibrant, and caring woman Grace once was all those years ago before the foster home had been all but forgotten. She spent her mornings staring into the yard and letting her coffee get cold. She began to stop holding herself responsible for the children and the chores she needed to do around the house. All the work suddenly fell onto the nanny's shoulders.

CHAPTER 7

"Hey Ben, wait up!"

Isaiah caught up to him in the hallway at school. He grabbed his shoulder, pulled him in, and hugged him.

Ben was confused and a bit weirded out. "What are you doing?" He pushed Isaiah off him. Isaiah, being too strong for him, pulled him back in and hugged him tighter.

"I will always be with you and never abandon you, no matter what," Isaiah said, pointing to Benjamin's chest.

"Yo, you're acting weird, bro." Ben looked startled. He couldn't help but stare into Isaiah's eyes. They were pure and true; he meant every word that he said.

The second bell rang, signaling they were late. They simultaneously—almost instinctively—smiled and bumped fists before turning their separate ways to go to class. Isaiah smiled for the rest of the day. Ben smiled when no one was looking.

On this particular day, the weather was gorgeous, and every kid in the house voted to go to the community pool. The community pool was actually three large swimming pools, with plenty of room for plenty of people. By this time, Ben's constant training regime inspired by Isaiah's natural frame had given him confidence. Benjamin was small but he had impressive lean muscle that left no room for fat. The nanny drove the kids to the pool while Grace and Matthew stayed home to drink.

"Wow," Alyssa said.

"I know, right?" exclaimed Daisy.

"Isaiah is still bigger though."

"Well, obviously." All the girls laughed together.

"What's so funny?" John tried to chime in.

"Who asked you, John?" Victoria shot back.

"Well, I just heard—"

"Why are you forcing yourself into our business? Go back to your underground market that you run at school," Daisy said, interrupting him mid-sentence.

The girls laughed together at John. John grew as red as a tomato. However, he recovered quickly, back to his paper white skin. Then, he scoffed at the girls.

Most of the boys were out at the furthest pool playing Marco Polo. Ben and Isaiah were trying to see who could do a better flip into the pool. The girls were admiring the two as they laughed together. "Wait!" Ben paused and acted like he was looking into the water. "Close one." The lifeguard's peering eyes almost caught them doing a backflip.

"We have got to do it without a run-up. It's the only way."

"Agreed," Isaiah confirmed.

"So hot." The girls continued drooling from the other pool.

"But why does he have to be such an asshole all the time?" asked Victoria.

"I know, like, I didn't realize men had periods, too!" Alyssa said. They laughed again. John joined in the laughter, still hanging around them.

"Why are you still here?" Alyssa asked.

"Why are you?" She scoffed and gave a threatening look. "Just go away."

John ignored them. He walked around them as if he were studying them. "So, you like watching them shirtless?" he deduced.

"John, no one is talking to you. Just go away," Victoria said.

"You are right now! Why do you girls even like them? They are ugly and weird. Isaiah smells bad, too."

"No, John, you smell. You're weird and you're ugly." All the girls laughed at John again.

"Ugh." He paused. "Lifeguard!" John called out. The lifeguard looked over with a whistle in his mouth. "Those two are doing flips in the pool!" he said, pointing at Ben and Isaiah.

The lifeguard looked at them. The two threw their hands up in confusion, attempting to avoid suspicion. The lifeguard sighed, dropped the whistle from his mouth, and yelled, "No flips." He put the whistle back between his teeth and adjusted his sunglasses as he leaned back in his tall, white chair. John walked away from the girls and then passed the two boys; they were like predators crossing paths.

"Damn, now we can't do flips without being caught."

"I know. It's unfortunate."

"John's a prissy, bitchy, pasty albino." Ben smiled as he said it.

"Actually, albinos would have colorless hair as well as a paler complexion. It's an extremely rare, lifelong condition where the genes involved in—" Isaiah was cut off.

"Agh, stop being annoying. I hate when you do that shit."

Isaiah went silent then changed the subject. "What should we do now?"

"Hmm. I don't know."

"Remember that guy who—" again, Isaiah was interrupted before he could finish.

"What guy? There are a lot of guys."

"The guy we saw when we closed the door to the house the other day."

"Remind me."

"I think his name is Keith Christ. The guy everyone talks about. The ginger whose beard doesn't connect but he's like fifty. Always mumbling to himself about nonsense. Sometimes we see him when we get off the bus."

"Oh, that drunk crackhead we saw!"

"Yes."

"I'mma just call him KC."

They laughed together. "You will do as you please," Isaiah added.

"What's that supposed to mean?"

"Nothing really."

They left the massive community pool area and slipped out without anyone noticing them. The two still had bathing suits on and a damp T-shirt. They both had a pair of all blue off-brand slides that were slightly too big and tripped them up as they walked. The pool was about two and a half miles from the house. By the time they made it onto the road, their shorts were entirely dry.

Back at the Edith house, the guilt and shame both Grace and Matthew were experiencing brought them together. The Edith couple sat down in the living room and took the time to talk it out.

"I'm sorry," Grace started.

"I am, too."

"I haven't been myself and I've hurt everyone. I can't seem to handle my emotions anymore. I'm up and I'm down; my impulses are all over the place." Grace began to cry. "And the alcohol just makes it worse. For me, but especially for you, Matthew. It has to stop."

"I'm sorry for letting it get this far. I don't want to keep messing things up with you and the kids. I don't want to ever lose you, Gracie. So, I agree, we need to be better, for us and for the kids."

"Together, for us and for the kids."

"Together." Matt smiled and embraced Grace, cherishing the moment.

The couple grabbed all the drinks from around the house and poured all the alcohol down the drain, signaling the return of the dream they had dreamt together: the loving Edith home for children.

The two boys stared as KC slept unbothered behind a dumpster. The shade of a pine tree kept him cool. He seemed happy. Benjamin started throwing tiny pebbles at his face.

"Stop that."

"Why?"

"It's mean."

"No, it's funny. Look, I bet I could get one in his mouth."

KC was sleeping with his mouth slightly open as he faintly snored. Ben threw a couple more pebbles until one bounced off his nose, onto his lip, and rolled into his mouth. The two boys began laughing as soon as it went inside. With lightning speed, KC shot up and got close to the boys. He spit the pebble into Isaiah's face, with a huge smile on his own and said, "Congratulations, you're a winner!"

The boys, startled, fell back onto the ground and locked up at the crazed man. Their roles had been completely reversed in a matter of seconds. KC looked down at them, still smiling. Then, he looked up and around, stretched big, and yawned.

"Pretty nice day huh?" KC said with a deep breath. The boys did not respond. "However," KC continued, "Shame it will never be as nice as the first days."

The boys were more confused than ever before. The listened as the freckled man torqued his head side to side, talking to himself.

"Yes, but with shame there is glory!" KC went on. "And with glory there is majesty." KC smiled at the boys again. "Peace be with you." Then, he walked away, seemingly still intoxicated from whatever he had earlier. The boys watched as KC walked away, crossed the street, and then disappeared into a hiking path in the woods. Then, the two boys burst into laughter.

"What the hell was that?" Ben exploded. "Yo, that's a weird dude!" Ben was hunched over in laughter, laughing so hard it was a workout.

"Definitely odd," added Isaiah.

"Look, he left a beer," Ben pointed out, controlling his emotion.

"Don't. Ben, that's nasty."

"Why? It hasn't been opened yet."

"It's all warm and gross and what if he's coming back for it?"

"He probably will, but it's all mine now."

Ben picked up the beer, cracked it open, and began walking toward the house. He took a sip of it as it pooled around the top of the cap. Then, he took a gulp so it wouldn't spill. "I've tasted better."

Isaiah ignored him. Ben finished the beer by the time they reached the house. He tossed it in the garbage cans by the mailbox. They walked back inside and went upstairs to the room. Isaiah was clearly bothered by Ben's behavior but decided to let it go.

"Yo, that guy KC was super weird," Ben started.

"Definitely interesting to say the least."

"Like, what was he even talking about? Like, what first days? And how can shame bring glory? Shame gets you alone, with no friends. Probably why he is alone with no friends."

"Why're you so mean? I'll be his friend," Isaiah defended. "Plus, I think you're looking too deep into this."

"You're weird, too!" Ben laughed.

Isaiah smiled. "Yeah, I am pretty weird." Isaiah felt warm and happy all of a sudden. He didn't mind that Ben had the last can of beer, even though he still thought it was a bad idea. Something about it just didn't sit with Isaiah, even though nothing bad happened. They talked mindlessly for hours until they both fell asleep and Isaiah decided to forget all about it.

Matthew came home late from a short trucking job. He was covering someone's shift for extra money on a six-wheeler. Since they had both vowed to stop drinking, Matthew hadn't been able to put his finger on an incredible itch travelling through and across his body.

Matt pulled in the driveway of their home and parked. He happened to see the beer can that Ben had left in the trash as he was checking the mail. Instead of going inside, Matthew hopped back into his beat-up truck and placed the mail on the passenger seat. He turned the key to start the engine back up, then sat there as the engine hummed. His thoughts were battling over whether he should head to the bar to drink or whether he should keep his promise to Grace this time around. It was as if a mighty war between angels and demons was taking place inside his head as he stared empty minded at the front door of his house. After waiting a few minutes, he put the car in reverse and backed out. Then, he drove off, not sure whether he wanted the angels to win this time. Seeing the beer can in the garbage sparked his deeply ingrained thought process of temptation, which led to him to desperately needing a drink. He knew it was wrong, but he knew it would make him feel the way he wanted to. Twenty minutes later, he returned with liquor and two six-packs. Stumbling inside, all he could focus on was drinking. He slept on the couch after hiding the liquor in the top cabinet. After what seemed like the blink of an eye, he awoke to the sound of children screaming as they ate breakfast.

Matthew groaned as he sat up and placed his hand on his head trying to control his pounding headache. The nanny passed by as he woke; instead of saying good morning, she just shook her head.

"What?" Matthew was confused.

The nanny kissed her teeth and left the room. Matthew knew what. He knew he drank four beers before coming home last night and then had two more on the drive. He knew he had four shots before putting the liquor away. He knew he finished his second six-pack and left the cans under the couch, some sticking out. He knew he wasn't hiding it and he knew that she knew.

The day continued without a fuss, simply because Matt drank himself into a midday nap and Grace's inner battles left her too exhausted to deal with the children. She looked as if she had aged three years in the past few months. The nanny asked for a raise and was granted one. She was fine with the drama, as long as she was being paid well for it. She actually didn't mind taking on all the kids; it wasn't so hard for her. They listened more to the nanny than they did their foster parents anyway, and a few of the boys even had a crush on her.

As time went on, Matt continued picking up some shifts here and there to avoid the house more. By God's will, he was never pulled over and never got into any accident while driving the trucks.

"What should I do?" asked Grace.

"What can you do?"

"Nothing! He won't listen to me."

"Honey, he is hot. There is no doubt about that. He's also getting a beer belly and his face is starting to sag. He's a mess and a drunk, leave his ass. Drop that man."

"Drop him? Are you crazy? I love him, even with all his imperfections. Sometimes he gets too drunk and sometimes he isn't caring but everyone has their flaws. We built this home together—a loving home. We are raising these kids together."

"Oh really?" Christina laughed. She had tan skin and thin black hair. She was extremely Italian, which was obvious with her not so subtle accent and the way she talked with her hands. "Together? Together! You two have not done shit together since you got this damn house. The last time we talked it seemed like he was making no effort at all! I know for damn sure that you're the only reason that house hasn't crumbled into ashes."

"Well. He has gotten better."

"The drinking though? Has that gotten better? No, that's gotten worse honey, way worse."

"You're right." She sighed.

"Drop him. Matthew is ruining your life and probably the lives of your kids, too."

"Christina! You're going too far. You know he's a good father to those kids."

Christina didn't stop. "I just hate to see you like this. Ever since you decided to do this thing—get all these kids and try to be Supermom—you have only gotten hurt and have only added more stress to your life. I want what's best for you, honey. I'm only telling you the truth, you know that."

"Yeah, yeah."

"I'm your best friend. I'll always give it to you straight."

"Well, maybe coat it with some love, will ya?"

"I have! But this has gone on for too long, Grace. I don't want you to turn into some old grouch who hates life and complains all the time. We are supposed to retire and get a beach house together, remember? So, stop taking on kids, will ya?" She laughed.

"Ohh, you know I won't. I'm too proud to be a complainer. Yes, that's still the plan." Grace smiled. She loved Christina, probably more than anyone in the world. They had known each other since high school and while Christina lived in California, she still came out to visit when she could. "Thanks for coming to see me, Christina. You are my best friend; that's for certain. Anyways, I gotta get back now. It was great to see you. Will I see you soon?"

"Of course, honey! Love ya!"

They smiled together. Grace stood and hugged Christina. She left her in the outdoor restaurant they were eating at and headed back home in an Uber. She got home to find Matthew on the same damn spot on the couch where she left him, sleeping again.

"I'm thinking about divorcing him."

"Divorce?" the nanny asked.

"Yes, divorce. It's not working out."

"What about all these years and money spent together? What about me and my job? What about these kids? Do you want to do that to these kids!"

"No, of course not. Calm down."

"Calm down? You can't do this, Grace, not now. You're in too deep now."

"Everything I do is for these children!" Grace yelled in defense.

The nanny lowered her tone to an almost soft whisper, "Then do what's right for these kids."

"I have been, I swear. I have been."

"I know you have. I'm here with you in the thick of it. You must continue. What Matthew does is horrible and cannot be excused. But these kids don't need that. They deserve better. They came here for better lives. Don't ruin that for them."

"Yeah." She sighed. "Yes, you are right," she repeated more sternly. Then, she laughed and said, "All except that wretched Benjamin."

"That child is the spawn of Satan." They both laughed together and connected deeper.

"It's probably because of what happened to him."

The nanny agreed. "Still, Ben and Matthew always know how to fuck shit up. That's for certain." They continued to laugh together, all the while talking shit, assuming that no one was home.

However, someone *was* home. Two other people were home, and the two women didn't seem to realize. Matthew laid on the couch half asleep, listening in. At the top of the stairs was Benjamin, crouched down and eavesdropping, as well. He had skipped school and hid in his room. He even called in sick for himself so there would be no suspicion; he just wanted to be alone. Isaiah told him it was a bad idea, but he did not heed. But in that moment, he wished he had. He grew angry. He felt betrayed by the ones who were meant to take care of him. He felt discarded and more alone than ever. He hated his foster parents and that sneaky nanny, too. Matthew grew more depressed and more inward; it only fueled his desire to drink himself through the days.

CHAPTER 8

Halloween arrived and the children were all ready to go. Jayden wasn't participating in the holiday. Instead, he spent his time studying in his room. All Jayden wanted was to escape the reality that he lived in and find something better. Actually, he wanted to find *somewhere* better. Patrick, the second oldest, was already long gone, trick or treating with his friends from school. Patrick didn't care about being in a foster family either. He was just content with the hand he was given in life and didn't try to fight it.

Pablo dressed as a flower, which was an odd choice in the eyes of all the other children. Eyebrows raised as Pablo descended the stairs, proudly wearing his flower outfit. He was finally stepping out of his comfort zone. The kids looked away and started laughing. Pablo's confident aura had turned gloomy.

Shawn jumped to his defense. "I think you look good."

"Me too!" added Alyssa.

"Yeah." Daisy leaned in and whispered, "Screw those guys; you're doing great."

Pablo teared up and smiled, "Thank you, guys. I actually made it myself."

"What? That's amazing! I couldn't even tell. It looks expensive," said Daisy.

Pablo blushed and then got his candy bag from the nanny.

John dressed as a pimp. He came downstairs in fake gold chains and a backwards cap. His pants were too long for him and sagged nearly to his thighs. He paired them with a baggy t-shirt to complete the look. It didn't last long, though. He was forced to change.

Benjamin was dressed asa devil, and when the nanny asked him to change, he downright refused. The nanny asked Grace to handle it because she was tired of trying to reason with him. Grace attempted to get him to remove the outfit. He stared defiantly into her eyes, almost pushing his chest at her.

"No." He walked away.

Finally, the two adults brought Matthew, the "dominant presence," into the situation. But Matthew did not care; he was simply trying to appease his wife and the finger pointing nanny.

"Uh, hey, Ben. Why are you wearing that?" He got on one knee and lowered himself to Ben's level.

"Because they told me to."

"They told me they are telling you to change, actually." Matthew was confused.

"They did."

"So, why haven't you?"

"They called me the spawn of Satan, so that's how I'll dress." Ben looked at the floor, not ashamed of his outfit, but rather ashamed that he was a part of this foster family.

"Oh." Matthew, taken aback, stood. He looked over to the two other adults. He saw Grace and the nanny talking in whispers in the other room. Matthew remembered what they had said. He had been so focused on the comments made towards him that he didn't put much thought into what they said about Ben.

"Wear whatever you want to wear." He smiled. Ben smiled back and walked to the front door where the rest of the kids were getting ready.

"Did you tell him?" Grace appeared out of nowhere behind Matthew as he watched Ben trail away.

"Yeah, I told him."

"So why isn't he getting changed? That's not how he should dress."

"Why not?"

"Because he is dressed as adevil! That is unacceptable."

"A lot of things are unacceptable. But they still happen."

"What do you mean?"

Matthew scoffed and turned away.

Grace showed interest in Matthew only because she had interest in hearing more.

"Baby, what is it?" She caressed his shoulder and turned him to her.

"Don't baby me. You're fake. Ben and I both heard what you had to say."

"Excuse me?"

"You're excused." Matthew retired to his room, leaving her speechless.

John came back downstairs with an almost identical outfit on.

"John, what did I say?" asked the young nanny.

"I did. I changed. This time, I'm a rapper."

The nanny didn't care too much and simply didn't want to be bothered anymore so she let it slide.

Isaiah was dressed asa web-slinging superhero; his muscles stretched the fabric to its limit.

"Are you sure you're comfortable? You could wear this costume instead.. He's cool, too."

A bunch of costumes were given to the Edith house as a donation. Even though they had plenty of money, they graciously accepted the gifts. Grace had already asked Isaiah once before, but the outfit was so tight she felt bad and couldn't help but ask again.

"You said to pick your favorite, right?"

"That is correct," Grace sighed with a smile.

"Then I am very comfortable."

"Okay then, Isaiah, whatever you prefer."

She then turned away to address the others. Shawn was dressed as a red crayon, his orange hair adding to the effect. Jack was a silver ninja with plastic shurikens. Jimmy didn't know what to be so the nanny chose for him. He wore fake glasses, a red beanie, jeans, and a white and red striped shirt. She was aiming for him to bethe impossible boy to find, from the popular children's puzzle book series. . Jimmy didn't get it and didn't know who the character was, but he wore the costumeanyway. Vinny dressed as his favorite superhero, the humble protector dressed all in black. .

"Grace?" Vinny pulled on her.

"Yes, Vinny, what's wrong?"

"Why isn't Patrick here?"

"Patrick is out with his friends this year."

"Aren't we his friends?"

"Yes, but he has other friends, too. He wants to spend time with all his friends."

"Oh, okay." He sighed. "He should be here, though."

"I know, I know. But let's still have a lot of fun, okay? And get a lot of candy!" She lowered her voice like a monster as she yelled. All the kids yelled with her for a second shout.

The entire foyer was filled with children chanting, "Candy, candy, candy!"

In his room, Jayden's eyes twitched, and he slammed his fist on his bed. Then, he calmed himself and put headphones on. Matthew was on the toilet with his hands over his ears.

"Let's go trick or treat!"

"Yeah!" All the kids shot through the front door like water from a busted pipe.

The children ran all around through the night, filling their bags to the brim. Each child brought an extra bag for when theirs got too full; however, the nanny refused to carry any candy bag. She was carrying enough already; she needed her one hand ready, predicting Vinny would want to be picked up sooner or later. Almost all the kids stayed together, except the ones who cared more for trouble than they did for candy.

When there was a chance Benjamin, Jimmy, Isaiah, Daisy and Alyssa all ran away. Using trails through the woods, they made it far from the rest of the group and were headed to another neighborhood. Daisy was dressed an ice princess, pretending she could control the ice and snow with her mind like a witch.

"Chill, let me walk."

"C'mon Satan. Don't you think you can beat a witch?"

"Stop," he sneered.

"Loser." Daisy tripped him and he landed in the dirt as she walked away. Ben wanted to be angry at her but for some reason he wasn't.

The little police officer was Alyssa, who tried countless times to arrest the boys during their journey through the woods, especially Spiderman.

"Hands in the air, web-slinger!"

"My hands are in the air."

"You're under arrest."

"For what, Officer?"

She walked behind him and pulled his hands down. Alyssa slowly put her handcuffs on Isaiah. As she clicked it in place, she whispered in his ear so no one else could hear. Isaiah's eyes grew wide, and he smiled even wider. She pushed him forward down the path.

Still with the pack was Victoria who was dressed as a mermaid. They never even realized that the troublemakers had left. Victoria was walking and talking with John, his fake plastic chains swinging from side to side. She filled John's mind with school drama and her problems during class. John listened because she was his sister but he certainly wasn't entertained.

The group of five reached the next neighborhood and blended in with the crowds of trick or treaters.

"Let's play ding-dong-ditch," Daisy recommended to her small group of delinquents.

"How? It's Halloween," added Alyssa.

"What's ding-dong-ditch?" asked Isaiah.

"Why would you ask?" Alyssa cried out.

Daisy began laughing menacingly, "Follow me, I'll show you." She giggled.

"You're crazy," added Ben.

"You don't know half of it," Alyssa said.

"Shhhh." Daisy laughed as she motioned Alyssa not to say anything more.

"Whatcha mean? Tell me!" Ben insisted.

"Daisy is insane, one time..."

"Stop!" yelled Daisy.

"It's not a bad one, I promise." Daisy gave her a look and allowed her to continue. "One time, during class, while the teacher wasn't looking, Daisy shot a spitball at the back of her head. It was so funny, oh my gosh." Daisy was laughing with her.

"Oh, perfect! Here! Here is a good one!" Daisy changed the topic, pointing to a house.

"Why is that a perfect one?" asked Ben, confused.

"Because you can see the people are awake. They clearly aren't celebrating Halloween. There isn't one decoration or even a bowl of candy left out. You can see them watching TV through the window."

Isaiah and Alyssa peered through the small window, confirming Daisy's observations.

"So, how is that perfect?" Isaiah asked.

"Because it is clear that they don't want to be bothered." Daisy began laughing. "But we are gonna ring the doorbell so many times they have to get up." She laughed even harder. "Plus, we can hide behind this big bush."

"Hide?" Ben was confused.

"Yeah, we ring the doorbell, run away, and hide. Then, we laugh at the angry old man that hates kids and has to answer the door."

"But this guy actually hates kids. I know, I've met him before. I've seen him here."

"Yeah, duh, that's what I just said."

"Okay then, whatever you say, Daisy."

The five young children hid behind the large shrubbery and mentally prepared themselves for what would unfold. They hid so no stray trick or treaters could see them either, although they were at a strip of houses that clearly did not celebrate Halloween.

"Leave it up to Daisy to find the perfect place to ding-dong-ditch." Daisy bowed with a smile.

"Who should go?" Isaiah asked.

"Isaiah, you go!" Alyssa laughed.

"Why Isaiah?" Daisy seemed hurt.

"He's the fastest. Plus, you've done this before. He hasn't," returned Alyssa.

"Huh? No, I am the fastest," said Ben interrupting. Isaiah said nothing.

Alyssa laughed, "Sure ya are, Ben. Sure ya are."

"So, who is going?" Daisy asked.

It was silent for a minute, but it felt like hours to the kids.

"Isaiah is going, like I said."

"Isaiah?" Daisy asked Isaiah, waiting to see his response.

"Sure, I'll go."

Isaiah calmly removed himself from the group and awkwardly walked up to the house. He came to the door and rang the bell; then, he calmly jogged away back to the group. He took his time sitting back down and seemed to have no sense of urgency. They all waited in anticipation, glaring through the foliage. Nothing happened.

After a few minutes, Daisy grew impatient. "Did you actually ring the bell?"

"Yes, obviously."

"It's not obvious. The guy didn't answer the door. Isaiah, ring it again. Ring it a bunch of times and bash on his door, too."

"Okay, I guess."

Isaiah approached the house again. This time, he was a bit on edge. He rang the bell profusely, at least ten times. Then, he knocked on the door like an officer with a warrant. He dashed back to the bush and sat next to Alyssa, nudging up against her. They were all glaring at the door. Within ten seconds, an overweight man opened the door already furious. He yelled, "I have no damn candy for y'all." He looked all around, surveying his front yard. "Try that again, ya shitheads! You'll be sorry." He turned back inside and slammed the door behind him.

The group of five listened silently. The moment he was inside and the door shut, they all began laughing, rolling on the grass and holding their guts.

"Did you see him wobble like a penguin!" Daisy yelled. They all laughed harder.

"He looked mad. We should stop." Isaiah wasn't laughing anymore.

"Yeah, he did," Ben agreed, but he was laughing hysterically, enjoying the man's irritation and focusing solely on his own pleasure. "I wanna do it this time."

"Alright." Daisy was smiling like the Grinch. "I know another good house to hit."

"I wanna do this one again," Ben said.

"This one? That's risky."

"That's the point."

Ben got up without waiting for a response. He ran up to the door and rang the bell like a mad man. He sprinted back and slid into his hiding place. Just as he got there, the man opened the door again. His face was red from anger. He was on the phone while holding a bat. He hung the phone up, slipped it into his pocket, and put two hands on the bat. Squeezing the bat, he yelled into the dark night. "I called the cops! Y'all in trouble now!"

"Oh no." Alyssa went white in the face.

"It's okay," Daisy said, calming her. "Let's just leave now. He's probably bluffing."

The group of five left. Ben was proud of his act, and they continued to ding-dong-ditch, hitting every house they could down the block that would lead them back to their neighborhood. They ding dong ditched as many houses as they could. All five got a turn, Jimmy was almost caught but they all ran away laughing all the way.

"Told you I'm the fastest," Ben said ahead of the group.

"Isaiah wasn't even trying," Added Alyssa, then she grew red.

"Well, I still am," Ben announced.

The five kids ravaged the neighborhood until they eventually got bored and returned to the main pack with the rest of the foster children from the Edith house. By this time, they had done a loop of the neighborhood. When they merged back with the group, everyone just assumed they had run ahead. The five who returned still managed to fill their bags with candy, calling the day a success.

All the children returned home with a smile on their faces. Jayden was done studying; he was present and talkative when the kids returned. Jayden bartered for some Snickers, his favorite treat. However, it was still clear the Jayden was not happy nor friendly. At that point, he was simply surviving.

The Edith house was pulsating with noisy, sugar-filled children. Matthew was upstairs in his room with the door shut, drinking again. Grace and the nanny were downstairs with the children conversing and comforting them as they shared in their Halloween spoils.

Everything was going well. The kids were all beginning to wind down. Grace was asleep, Vinny was knocked out, and the girls were all gathered in their room.

Matthew came downstairs looking for a snack in his drunk state of mind. He clamored down the last steps and dragged his feet as he walked to the kitchen. The nanny was in the kitchen with Shawn. He wanted a glass of warm milk to wash down all the sugary treats he had. Shawn waited as the nanny heated the milk in the microwave, still holding his pillowcase filled with candy.

Matthew did not say a word to either one; instead, without asking, he reached into Shawn's bag and took a massive handful of the candy. Once Shawn realized, he began yelling at his foster father, claiming he took his favorite ones. Matthew ignored him and walked away, back to the stairs. He grunted as he stumbled up the stairs, swinging with each unstable step. Shawn began crying. In fact, he cried all throughout the night.

The next day, three neighbors and another two from the town over showed up at the door threatening to press charges because they kids were playing ding-dong-ditch several times throughout the night. Their claims were supported by the local kids and the entire block they had raided. Not only did they suspect Edith's foster kids, but they even pointed them out.

Daisy, Benjamin, Isaiah, Jimmy, and Alyssa were the culprits in question. They were pinpointed by their costumes. Daisy and Benjamin flat out denied it, Isaiah answered no questions, and Jimmy and Alyssa avoided the truth. However, after immense pressure, Jimmy folded, spilling all the beans. Although the community gave the group of five just a slap on the wrist, Grace punished them by taking away some playtime and replacing it with more chores. Benjamin and Isaiah were the ones that were blamed for the whole thing, and they received most of Grace's wrath on a daily basis. Daisy was still considered an angel, Jimmy was simply too young to be blamed, and Alyssa was a great brown-noser; she knew how to get on Grace's good side.

CHAPTER 9

From all the foolishness from the kids and the drunkenness from the parents, the house was a terrible place to live. The constant immaturity and degenerate activity of the young boys only made it worse. It was as if celebrating Halloween that year had let in a swarm of evil entities that aimed to kill, steal, and destroy all that the Edith's had worked for. With lost hope that their relationship would be resurrected again, Grace and Matthew grew distant. The pillars of the house fell yet somehow, it still stood, creaking with the wind ready to collapse at any point. The Bible verses that had once populated the house were nowhere to be found. Grace didn't like to be reminded of God anymore. She hid the frames and abandoned them. And so, God abandoned the house and let all the evil spirits roam free. There was no more guidance; sin overtook the household and latched onto the children like a leech. The nanny tried her best but there was only so much she could do in the midst of such chaos.

The foster parents tried many times to get rid of Benjamin, who they thought was the instigator of it all, but nothing was working. They tried to get him adopted, but no one wanted him. Tried to get him transferred, but it didn't work. Tried to force him into submission, but there was no hope. That just made the boy even more restless.

The only adult to ever calm Benjamin down, commune with him, and understand him was the local crackhead, Keith Thomas Christ Jr. Everyone knew of him, but no one dared to talk to him. But Ben and

Isaiah didn't see him as dangerous but rather as a friend. They visited him despite being punished for it every time. They had met Mr. Christ the day Ben threw a pebble in his mouth. KC was their only escape from their cold reality, where fear was so strong you could smell it in the air. He didn't act the same with them as he did with others. When the three were together, they were their freest selves; Benjamin smiled and Isaiah talked, all while they listened to the random bursts of thoughts from the local crackhead. Whenever the boys visited KC, he would never be a bad influence, although he surely looked like he could have been.

The boys made it a routine to visit him every Sunday, a day they had nothing to do but chores. The two boys felt safe with him and showed the small amounts of hidden joy that was still left in them. Although KC didn't know the details of their lifestyle, he knew that they were mischievous children, and he didn't care. They always approached him with a glow, almost like he could see their happiness being worn like a garment. Seeing the two boys every Sunday brought KC immense happiness in the wake of his loneliness.

In the cold, fearful house, the rough treatment the children were getting was beginning to become unbearable. They were treated like animals, being smacked around for minor things like not making their bed. Their foster mother would punish them by starving them or keeping them in their rooms for days on end.

"Get your ass back here!" screamed their foster father.

"Nah, nah nah, nah, nah, nahhhhhh. You can't catch me!" Ben taunted him, shaking his hips.

"I'm gonna beat your little—aaaaahhhhhh!" Matthew caught his feet on a rope secured by the closet door. Daisy smiled as she pulled the rope in preparation, sending their father plummeting to the ground. It was no thin rope; he would have recognized it if he weren't black out drunk again.

"Loser," Ben said, holding up an L as he, Daisy, and Isaiah scurried away and turned the corner.

Although their foster parents were harsh, the boys didn't help their case much. They were always setting up devious pranks and causing chaos in the house. Grace had been leaving the house more often and no one knew why. Not even the nanny. Victoria was convinced that she left the house so she could cry alone in peace.

There had been a lot of nights like this lately, where the nanny tried to take care of the young children while the troublemakers pissed off drunk Matthew and Grace was nowhere to be found. There wasn't much the nanny could do to stop it. Half the time she wasn't even sure who was responsible for all the chaos, and didn't know who to punish.

One foggy day, on April 16th, 2018, it was John's fourteenth birthday. Obviously, the kids didn't like John much, since he was the goody two-shoes of the house and the tattle tale. He managed to get away with everything while always getting others in trouble. Benjamin was setting up the day so absolute chaos would erupt, which is when he would finally exact his revenge for all that John had got him into trouble for.

A large overhang canopy was set up in the yard for John's birthday. The weather channels were reporting rain, and they prepared for that. Thankfully, the skies were cloudy, but it didn't pour. Ben had been up all night, tying a small rope to a leg of the tent. The other side of the rope trailed inconspicuously to the lawnmower, hidden at the side of the house next to the shed. While it wasn't much to set up, the planning took a while.

What happened next went exactly according to plan. The party began the next day at around noon. A few hours went by and the time for the birthday cake rolled around. After begging Isaiah for hours to join him in his master plan, he finally agreed. Isaiah asked to use the bathroom and went to the side yard just as the cake was being set in front of John. John's wide eyes were captivated by the glowing flames of the candles as he basked in his glory and attention. Isaiah had walked to the shed and turned the lawnmower on right as everyone had finished singing happy birthday, masking the sound with all the claps. In an instant, the furthest tent leg was pulled through quickly and forcefully by the tightening rope, completely collapsing the tent. It went tumbling down, broken tent legs and all.

Seeing the moment to strike, Ben, who was standing behind the wide-eyed John, shoved his face into the cake, squishing it and smearing it around, spilling vanilla frosting everywhere before getting caught. John almost suffocated from the frosting overload; Ben couldn't contain his joy of seeing John's big day go to hell.

Even when he was caught red-handed, he was not apprehended. Ben ran for his life after looking Grace in the eyes. He got out just as the tent encompassed all the party goers. In the commotion, Grace was pacing towards Ben and had fallen awkwardly after being slammed in the head by the metal supports of the tent that lost their integrity. She fell with her arm first. It landed right under her back and a big *snap* rang out. She screeched and screamed in pain. "My arm!"

Ben and Isaiah did not plan for this to happen. They only planned for John to be crying with cake all over his face. which *did* happen; however, this mission was far from a success story.

 Ben and Isaiah were punished severely. Grace's arm was broken even worse than they had thought—in four spots to be exact. She spent the next two days at the hospital. She returned home with a hard cast on and a sling for support.

She greeted all the children when she returned with a comforting smile. Ben and Isaiah were in their room when she walked inside. They could hear the noisy children welcoming her home. They began to sweat and shake in fear. Ben was biting his nails and Isaiah was staring at the wall. The boys were afraid for no reason. She didn't even bother to say hello, let alone reprimand them for all that they had put her through.

The rest of the week went surprisingly well. They were relieved from their profuse cleaning of the house and were allowed to roam again. The boys didn't care that it was odd; they ran out of the house the first chance they got. At the end of the week, however, their foster mother called them into her room, just the two of them. The two children reluctantly walked into her room, inching themselves forward, afraid of what was to come. She waited for them to shut the door behind them, then she stood from her desk.

"What you did was terrible." She shook her fist.

The room was silent. Ben's head drooped to the ground, and he stared at the floor. Isaiah was staring at Grace, directly in the eyes and unwavering.

"I have been trying even harder to get you little shits out of here, but nothing is working. I can't seem to rid myself of you two. You know, Isaiah isn't too bad. He just hangs out with the wrong people." She looked at Isaiah with pity, "But you!" she said, changing her attention to Benjamin, who still stared at the floor. "You, Benjamin, you're worthless! You will always be worthless. I wish some other family would take you already but you're such a damn reject that nobody wants you! Ha! Isn't that something?"

Ben couldn't lift his eyes from the floor, while Isaiah, with piercing dark brown eyes, kept staring into Grace's soul. He kept a straight face and a perfect posture. He gave no sign of any emotion yet the wild look in his eyes that would not stop staring gave Grace great fear.

"So, this is what we are going to do. I'm going to make you two go back to doing chores. I don't care what you do during the day. But before bed every night, I will check to make sure you did your jobs. If they aren't finished, I will drag you out of bed and make you finish them."

Ben picked his head up while she was talking, a disrespectful look brewing on his face. "But you and Matthew said that we were all done and we didn't have to anymore!"

Immediately, Ben was slapped across the face, leaving a harsh sting.

As Ben rubbed his red cheek, she yelled back at him. "Do I look like Matthew? No, I look like Grace! Shut up and do what I say. Now, get to work!"

They both stared at her and then stood in despair and disbelief, turning to walk out of the door.

"Now, you little shits!" she screamed in a fit of rage.

Grace grabbed them by their hair and dragged them out of her room, throwing them into the hallway and slamming her door. Ben and Isaiah knew they had no choice but to do as she said.

"What now?"

"Now, we go do our chores," Isaiah said.

They sat in the hallway, still on the floor where they had been thrown.

"I don't want to though," Ben said.

Isaiah looked at him. "Yeah but at least, in a way, we have more freedom now."

"That's true. So, now we can do our chores early and then do whatever we want for the rest of the day."

"That's a great idea."

They decided they would turn their despair into motivation. They planned to wake up early every morning and finish their chores quickly. This way, the rest of their day was free to visit Keith Christ, or simply get out of the house. Isaiah went to school and never had an absent mark. Ben stopped showing up to school all together; instead, he would roam town looking for things to do that excited him, like going sledding on a golf course or breaking into a movie theater.

As time went on, Ben started to wonder why he never got into trouble for skipping school every day. He contemplated the reasons with KC every now and then as they walked together through beaten down trails and kicked rocks. Ben assumed it was because his fosters parents had completely given up, but that didn't make sense because they still hated him and beat him often. KC suggested that Ben had a guardian angel, and in response, Ben suggested that KC should stop doing drugs. They laughed together and continued to talk.

Little did Ben know that Isaiah was redirecting the absent calls from school to a pizzeria nearby, so his foster parents never even had a clue that Ben hadn't been going to school. Since Ben always made sure to take the bus, the other kids never told on him, since they simply assumed that Ben wasn't in their classes. Plus, Isaiah was always covering for Ben.

Over one year had passed and this type of lifestyle became the norm. Life did not get easier, and the foster parents did not loosen the noose around their necks. Yet the children found fun in life and continued to grow as people.

Using their free time and knowing their only friend in the house was having a birthday soon, Benjamin stole an R rated movie from the local Blockbuster with Isaiah as his look-out. They hid the DVD until Daisy's birthday.

On July 1st, 2019, was Daisy's twelfth birthday. Daisy had her little birthday party during the day, like every foster child did. This was special though, something only Benjamin, Isaiah, Daisy, and Alyssa would share together. They were all starting to grow up, and this was a way to show that to each other—watching a scary movie when they weren't supposed to.

Isaiah still had a muscular frame looking far older than everyone else. Alyssa had grown taller than Ben and Daisy, as both Alyssa and Daisy began to mature. Ben looked the same as always, just with much longer hair.

Ben stole one of the cheapest horror movies in the store called *Death is Approaching*. After everyone had fallen asleep, they tip-toed downstairs to watch the movie on the living room couch. Thankfully, Matthew fell asleep in his own bed that night. Benjamin slowly inserted the DVD into the player. The machine gobbled it up and loaded the screen. They pressed play but made sure to keep the volume very low. The movie started and they munched on some of the snacks they'd prepared.

"Ew, look at that," Alyssa said.

They were all sitting on the old, musty and brown couch placed in front of the even older television. The poorly filmed movie was reaching a classic and excessively gory scene.

"That's sick," Ben mumbled.

"You're a weirdo," Daisy laughed.

One of the clueless teenagers in the movie ran into the killer, which resulted in her demise. The killer used an axe to cut into the teenager's skull, showing her head crack open like an egg. The effects were so obviously fake, and there was an unnecessary and even absurd amount of ketchup grade fake blood spraying from her head like a sprinkler. Ben laughed at the scene before him.

"Wait, you hear that?" Isaiah snapped.

Alyssa reached for the TV and turned the volume down even further.

"It's nothing. Turn it back up already," groaned Ben.

"Oh fine." She reluctantly turned it back up and sat back in suspicion.

As the movie continued to show the killer's bloodthirsty attempts at killing the teenagers, Grace headed towards them. She slowly finished her descent from the stairs and made her way to the living room like a house cat.

"What is going on here?" Grace roared into the living room, blasting fear into the children. They all froze, staring at Grace as her face seemed to grow as red as a tomato. They jumped off the couch. Isaiah turned the TV off. Ben and Alyssa were as pale as a ghost and profusely sweating; they knew they were done for.

"Ahhh shit," sighed Daisy.

They were all punished, but Daisy and Alyssa not so much. There was no fairness in the punishments Grace dished out. Ben's hate for his foster parents grew to an unhealthy extreme; he only knew disobedience.

CHAPTER 10

"Take that!" Ben exclaimed. He was throwing a heavy basketball around his room with Isaiah. Each miss would hit off their walls, ripping a piece of wallpaper and cracking the plain Sheetrock, as well. The wallpaper, a plain blue, was at least forty-five years old and peeling away at every corner. Although it was half past midnight, the room was illuminated with the light of the moon—just enough light to have some fun before bed.

The upstairs sounded like a stampede was running through it, as if the second floor would come crashing down like a sinkhole pulling in cars.

"I finally have some alone time. This is the one night I like to watch TV. I can't even have one damn night to myself because of these kids," Grace scoffed.

Matthew groaned and chugged the last few sips of his beer. He sat up from the couch, grabbing another scoop from his popcorn bowl. "I'll check it out."

"Yeah, you do that." Grace placed her glass of wine on the coffee table alongside the popcorn.

"No, now I don't want to."

"Asshole, why?"

"You know why." Matt didn't look at her; he plopped back onto the couch and placed the bowl of popcorn on his lap.

"Oh, fine then. I do everything in this damn house either way."

Slowly tip-toeing up, she barely made a sound with each step, thinking she could frighten the boys by catching them in the act of doing something they shouldn't be going yet again. She was pissed off and drunk, ready to discipline violently. They continued throwing around the waterlogged basketball that had been sitting in the backyard for the past two weeks. Isaiah dodged one throw and then ran to their door, backed up against it.

"Oh, I've got you now!"

Ben cranked back his arm, winding up for a powerful throw. Grace slowly opened the door outward to the hallway falling back. In that moment, Ben propelled the ball towards Isaiah as hard as he could. Ben overthrew the ball a bit upward aimed straight at their mother as Isaiah leaned into her legs, crouching her to the perfect bullseye. They both realized what they had done but it was too late.

Isaiah looked up as he fell backwards into his mother. He saw the ball travelling in slow motion towards her brittle body. The ball impacted her directly in the nose, immediately breaking it and sending a stream of blood gushing out. Grace was already mid-fall from Isaiah clashing into her legs and the raw power of the ball whipped her head, causing her to crash towards the floor. Her neck snapped on the corner of the wall, leaving her with an immediate concussion.

"No!" the boys screamed in terror.

They rushed to her side, knowing better than to touch her. Isaiah, for the first time, showed significant emotion as tears flowed from his eyes, fearing that Grace was badly hurt. Ben was also crying; however, he was more focused on himself and the punishment he'd surely receive rather than Grace's wellbeing.

Grace's nose quickly leaked out blood that slowly built up on her lips, pooling over into her mouth and down her cheeks. The ground beside her darkened with blood. She was frozen with lifeless eyes.

"What happened?!" screamed Matthew from downstairs.

"Hurry, Matthew! Call 911!" Isaiah yelled.

"I-I-I can feel muah bah hey." Her eyes were crossed and along with the blood, foam started spilling from her mouth.

Matthew immediately grabbed the phone, his hands shaking as he dialed 911. He requested an ambulance and then ran upstairs, still on the line.

"What have you two done…"

"We didn't mean to! We're sorry!"

"Excuse me sir? What is your emergency?" asked the operator.

"My-My wife, her neck. It's been broken." He knelt beside her, pushed the kids away, and leaned in. He checked her heartbeat and vision. "Her neck, the bone is sticking out. Oh my God."

"Sir, there is help on the way. Just wait there. Do not touch her; it could make things worse."

"Oh Lord, why?"

"Sir, can you tell me anything else?"

"Her nose is swollen and bleeding. She is foaming from the mouth. Please send help! Oh, Grace!"

"We are on the way, Sir. Hang tight! Who is home? My file says you run a group home?"

"Yes, everyone is home. Everyone is awake. Please hurry. "

He hung up and turned to two of his foster children, his calm and concerned face turning into hate and rage. Isaiah and Ben stood cold in their tracks, still in disbelief. The group of already frightened children who had left their rooms scattered like mice back in.

"Matt, we're sorry. We're sorry!"

"Sorry don't cut it!" He ferociously picked them up by their shirts, paced down the stairs, and smashed their legs and arms against the wall and railing.

"Let go!" They frantically yelped and squeaked for help, hitting his arms.

He wasn't fazed and didn't answer. Instead, his face flared red.

"No, please! Not again!" Ben cried. "I'm sorry, please! No! Sorry! Help! Someone help! We'll stop, okay? We'll stop! We'll stop! Whatever you want!" Ben screamed.

Matthew reached the entrance to the basement and took a step down. Isaiah stopped him as he held onto the ledge of the stairs with one hand and the other tightly embracing Ben's.

He didn't even register their pleas and cries. Instead, he pried Isaiah's hand off the top stair, swinging him down the stairs with Benjamin. They landed at the bottom of in the dark windowless cement room. They rolled in pain as blood leaked from their new gashes, pooling up with dirt from the musty cracked floor. They both got back to their feet, the adrenaline erasing the pain momentarily as they started sprinting to the top of the stairs where their foster father stood, staring down at them.

"Please, wait!" they yelled, stumbling up the stairs, reaching out with their arms.

He stood there with narrowed eyes looking down at them. 'Think about what you did."

He slammed the door shut just before they got to it and locked it. He faintly heard their cries. The basement was pretty soundproof. He backed up and turned toward the kitchen. His eyes were lifeless and seemed to have no emotion in them. He grabbed a glass from the cupboard and put it on the counter. Then, he went to the fridge, removed ice from the tray, and slid two cubes into the glass. He grabbed his whiskey and poured a hefty amount. After chugging the first two glasses, he poured another.

"What is going on? What happened?" the nanny emerged from her room.

"Grace. Ben and Isaiah, they might have killed her. I called the ambulance already."

"Oh my God. Where is she?"

"Upstairs."

"So, why the hell are you down here taking a shot?" She turned away in   disgust   and   ran   up   the   stairs.

"I, the kids. I was—ah, hell." He finished his drink in no hurry and decided to have another. After ten minutes, the ambulance arrived with no cop car.

"Where are the cops? I need them to watch the kids."

"A unit will be here any minute, Sir. You can meet us at the hospital when it arrives."

"I specifically called for a cop so this wouldn't happen!"

"I understand, Sir. We need to take her now."

"I'm coming. There is a nanny here that can watch them."

The EMTs looked at each other in confusion. After his temper tantrum, Matthew got into the vehicle and headed to the hospital with Grace, leaving his children behind with the nanny.

The boys were in the pitch-black cellar at the top of the stairs. After a while, they slowly made their way down and sat on the cold, dusty cement floor, huddling like penguins. The room smelled like pennies and old men with dried up blood all over the floor from previous beatings. It was damp and cold; the only things in the basement were a large closet, some garbage bags of clothes, and the boiler room.

"Isaiah?"

"Yeah?"

"I'm tired of this. I hate it here."

"I know, I know. Me too."

They huddled together, hugging as they were sitting, leaning on each other. Ben began to cry with a sniffle here and there.

"It's not fair. We didn't mean to. We were just messing around."

"I know. It was an accident."

"Fuck everyone. Fuck Matt! They suck. Everyone sucks."

"I suck?" asked Isaiah.

"No, you're the only person I will ever love."

"You love me?"

"Shut up."

"What?"

"I'm not weird. And don't be weird now."

"I didn't say you were. Why would I?"

They weren't crying anymore.

"Because I said that."

"So you meant it then?"

"Of course I did."

"I will never abandon you, Ben. I'll always be here for you."

They hugged once again, then turned and leaned on each other back to back, talking about KC, the weird crackhead they always had fun with.

"I'll get him back."

"Who?"

"Matthew."

"I don't think that's wise."

"I don't care."

Grace died the next week in the hospital, after a long, painful fight. The foster children mourned her death. Matthew was distraught and the house was silent. No one played games or ran around. No one did chores or made breakfast. The days after hearing the news were dark and gloomy. The house was cold and no heater could bring any warmth. They had a funeral and Matthew was a mess. He blamed Benjamin and Isaiah with every look.

It took a few months for the house to get busy again and for things to return to normal. He did not quit being a foster parent because it was always Grace's dream. He paid the nanny a lot more and expected more from. Surprisingly, though, he did a lot himself, as well—from housework to scheduling to instilling fear in the children so they would not cause trouble. It worked for the most part. Sometimes, the kids would act up but the house was a much calmer place now. Matthew felt as if he had put things in order—all things except Benjamin. It didn't matter how many beatings or how many times he left him alone in the basement; Benjamin would never listen. He was simply too stubborn.

Isaiah knew what he was getting into. He was still the smartest person in the house. Yet he continued to stay by Benjamin's side no matter what he did. Matthew could not stand them. He would yell at them and force them into the basement in the dark as he drank himself to sleep afterwards, sometimes forgetting them down there for days on end. The nanny saw what was happening and felt the urge to say something but the money she was making was not worth the risk. The foster children never seemed to genuinely smile again. They were constantly beaten down, both physically and emotionally. Matthew was clearly affected, as well; his sinister attitude carried over into his personal emotions so he would avoid his problems—avoid the heartbreak from losing Grace. Matthew would drink from dusk until dawn every day, somehow still managing to work around the house.

When the time came for the annual fourth of July fireworks, the boys were restricted from going, as promised. The plan was for Matthew to stay with the boys at home and the nanny to take the other children to see the light show. This was mainly because he wanted no responsibilities on a day that reminded him of Grace. He wanted to sleep in and drink his sorrow away all night—maybe beat Benjamin and Isaiah to let off some steam later.

The next couple of days leading up to July 4th, 2020 were terrible. They were filled with agony for Ben. Isaiah knew they would not go. For the first time in seven years, they wouldn't watch the fireworks. They were severely punished yet again, left with bruises and welts hidden under their clothes. Although they were both fourteen now, Matthew could not trust them alone. He slept in while the bus to take the others arrived at the house. Ben and Isaiah watched from their bedroom windows as the small bus pulled away and disappeared.

Benjamin refused to learn his lesson and mature; his stubbornness kept him and Isaiah from enjoying any time they spent there. And so, that night, Ben knew Matt was still sleeping and grew a massive urge to prank him. Even with Isaiah advising him not to, Ben glued Matthew's eyes shut while he slept. He used the superglue they had found in the cabinet downstairs, above the kitchen counter.

Their foster father awoke in fear an hour later, unable to open his eyes, no matter how much he tried. He fell from his bed and used his nightstand to stabilize himself. He was still a little drunk and definitely hungover. He stumbled to sit upright and weaved from side to side, experiencing a terrible migraine.

"Kids!" he screamed, hoping for a response. His voice cracked in fear.

Ben and Isaiah were still in their room, staring out the window and daydreaming. Matthew kept screaming and still received no response. As he stumbled through his doorway, he tried to get an idea of what was going on. He could see—just barely—out of his left eye. It felt like he was trying to look one-eyed through a screen door. He continued to call out as he used the wall to stabilize himself, still trying to open his eyes with his fingers, but it didn't work.

He mustered up the courage and began to seriously pry open his left eye, pushing through the pain. It wasn't glued as well as the right eye, so he aggressively forced it open. Each second he did, he experienced a higher degree of pain. As he pulled his eyelids apart, they began to stretch like bubblegum. He stopped; he was tearing up from the pain and breathing hoarsely. The tears helped a bit and he pulled them slightly apart, ripping his eyelashes off in the process.

At that point, he was standing in the middle of the hallway to the left of the stairs that he still could not see. He kept screaming for help, realizing no one was home.

"Pointless," he muttered. "Those rotten kids did this. And now they're hiding."

Matthew became engulfed in rage and used that power to pull his eyelids completely off of his eyeballs. He belched in pain as he did, and his eye began to bleed. Every time he blinked, his eye would get stuck again and he would have to re-open it. In the process, his vision would alternate from red to black.

Frustrated he could not get his vision back, he began to walk around near the stairs. He blinked again, shutting his eyes completely and cutting off his vision mid-step. He tried to regain his footing but instead, he stepped towards the stairs. He had nowhere to place his weight with his step, causing him to slip and fall. He landed on his back, which let out a loud *crack* as he began tumbling and rolling down. As he raced in somersaults to the ground floor, a small weight was waiting for him at the bottom of the stairs.

His head took all the impact of the fall, landing in a scorpion pose. His legs flew over his back and his face implanted into the weight at the bottom of the stairs, causing his head to crack open.

A broken back and ruptured skull killed Matthew. He sat there lifeless, in an unnatural position as if he were attempting some type of yoga pose. His arms flailed out like a bird or like a puppet in pain.

CHAPTER 11

"What was that?" Ben asked, startled by the noise.

"Let's check. It might be Matthew."

Isaiah sprinted down the old staircase with Ben following behind him. The two arrived at the second level and peered off the balcony, seeing Matthew leaking blood on the hardwood floor. They gasped in unison, both in complete disbelief. Benjamin completely froze; his muscles grew tense, and his body shook. Isaiah was thinking a million miles a minute as his eyes stared at Matthew's dead body.

Across town and far from the chaos brewing at the Edith house, the bus arrived at the picnic area. The nanny allowed the children to run amok as they pleased. They all got hot dogs and ice cream from a vendor. Gathered around an old, wooden picnic table, they prepared to watch the fireworks as the sun began to set against a cream orange sky.

Thick blood seeped into the creases of the hardwood floor. Ben threw up. His eyes began tearing up and he fell to his knees. His head began pounding like his heart was in his brain, tormenting his body and soul. Isaiah kept a cold stare, watching the lifeless body ooze blood.

Isaiah turned and sprinted back up to their room, leaving Ben dry heaving on the hallway floor. He grabbed the two duffle bags under his bed. He began stuffing all their clothes into the bags, along with any other memorabilia he could fit inside. Isaiah was talking to himself as he did all of this. "It's going to be okay. It's going to be okay. It's fine."

He finished packing and zipped up the duffle bags, then sprinted down the stairs. He saw Ben, wiping his mouth and still crying. Ben looked at Isaiah, his frown accompanied by a quivering lip and chin. His eyes squinted and he screamed in fright.

"What have I done?"

Isaiah came to his side and hugged him tight. "We will get through this. We will." He assured Ben over and over, trying to keep him in one piece.

As they approached the stairs, Isaiah grabbed some more essentials from the second-floor bathroom. He grabbed all he could see useful: a first aid kit from under the sink, two used sticks of deodorant, and a half empty tube of toothpaste. Isaiah stuffed them into the bag and dashed down the stairs, pulling Ben by the hand. Ben stumbled as he followed. When they reached the bottom of the stairs, both took turns carefully stepping over their foster father. Ben had his hand to his mouth and closed his eyes in disgust. He almost threw up on the carcass but he held it in, which left a bad taste in his mouth. Still, it was nothing like the rotten and sour taste of knowing he had just aided in someone's death. Again. Isaiah was still dragging Ben around as he rummaged through the coin jar in the kitchen.

He took all he could, dropping coins as he tried to shove them in the bag. He decided to just pour the entire jar into the bag. Then, he opened the pantry and filled up the last bit of room in the bags with non-perishables and canned food. Isaiah was pushing them off the shelf into the bag. In the process, the rice container fell to the floor, exploding upon impact, sending rice scattering all over the floor. Ignoring the mess, he zipped the bags up tight and tossed them over his shoulder. The coins chimed as he jogged to the backdoor with Ben. As they approached the door, Ben gripped the kitchen door frame, refusing to leave the house.

"No!" he screamed with a waterfall of tears pouring down.

"He's dead. Let's go, Ben," Isaiah responded softly.

"I just killed him. Do you know how much trouble I'm going to be in? What did we do?"

"You're not going to get in trouble because we're going to get out of here before anyone comes. There is nothing we can do to change what happened. We have to move on now. We cannot stay here anymore."

Ben understood and loosened his grip on the door frame. He took one last look at the man who raised them, his face still smashed into the ground and his legs in the air. The blood was thick and moved like molasses across the hardwood. Isaiah gave one more tug and Ben turned to him. They headed out the backdoor; Isaiah shut it behind them. He then stopped and stood still once they were outside. With wide, alert eyes, he took a deep breath and turned to Ben.

"Woah," he whispered.

Ben, now under control, mirrored Isaiah's emotion with an abrupt nod of his head and changed gears, focusing on their next move. They ran away from home with no intention of ever coming back. They left town, stealing Jayden and Patrick's bikes. By the time the firework show was over, it was dark, and the two boys were long gone.

The bus pulled into the driveway, squeaking as it eased into the driveway. All the kids jumped out of the bus screaming and yelling, having a great time. Even the nanny was living it up. She had already paid the bussing company and gave the man who drove them a tip. The bus pulled away as Victoria opened the front door. Six feet in front of her was her father's dead body and a dry pool of blood. She stood perfectly still.

"What's the hold-up?" Daisy asked, pushing inside. "Oh shit." She went still as well, then relaxed with a laugh. "Well, nice try. But that doesn't look like the movies at all, Matthew," she spoke with uncertainty. "I-I know you're faking it." Daisy hesitated.

Victoria began screaming and ran to call 911. A chorus of painful screaming bellowed from their souls, the scene scarring every child in that home.

The children were dispersed throughout the foster system once again and an intensive investigation began to understand what happened. The police tried to find and locate the two missing boys, hoping they'd be able to shed light on the case that seemed to be turning cold. No one knew what happened, and even the autopsy examiners couldn't imagine why or how this man was glued and eventually killed. There were no signs of foul play or forced entry. Besides knowing he fell down the stairs, they had no evidence that someone had done this to him. Detectives chased down every lead but ended up at multiple dead ends. Ben and Isaiah were not outlaws, but they were two undocumented suspects with the police and child services after them.

In four short months, it officially became a cold case and was eventually forgotten and thrown out. Isaiah and Ben were finally free from their ties and forged a new path for themselves. They were completely on their own for the first time and they burned any bridges that would lead them to their home.

CHAPTER 12

They took the train as far as they could. When they finally got off, the boys pretended to walk away. They waited for the peering eyes to go their separate ways, hopped over the fence, and began walking next to the train tracks. The crisp night air filled their lungs as they walked on the wet grass. The moon lit their way as if it weren't night; it was a quiet walk for them.

They walked for what seemed like hours. Out of boredom, they decided to see who was better at balancing on the train tracks. For miles, they walked on the beams with their arms out for balance. It smelled like pine, and they had no clue where they were. Yet they continued to walk, searching for a sign to a town or a city.

"Hey, Isaiah, are we criminals?" Ben asked, breaking the silence that was looming in the air.

"According to the law and according to religion, we are responsible for the crime, yet we ran away. So, yes, yes we are."

"Shut up! Just shut up, bro. It's so annoying when you do that."

"I'm only answering your question."

"Yeah, like a nerd. You're so annoying. You didn't even do shit anyways. It was all me. It's always me. You're still an innocent soul who always does what Mommy and Daddy tell you to do."

Isaiah stayed silent.

Ben wanted a comeback, but Isaiah remained calm. In frustration, he jumped into Isaiah, pushing him off the beam and into a thorn bush

"Who's annoying now?" Isaiah yelled as he sat in the bush.

"Wow, I got it to speak to me!" Ben looked around, addressing the imaginary crowd.

Isaiah got out of the bushes, carefully putting his hands through the open spots in the bush to help push himself up. The thorns were still stuck to his cotton black sweatpants, piercing into his elbows.

"Damn, my bad." Ben apologized as he bent down, helping to pull the thorn branches from his pants.

Isaiah looked up at him, his sky-blue eyes piercing through Ben's soul. "It's whatever. Just help me get these out; it hurts a lot."

"Yeah yeah, no problem."

Isaiah smiled. It was clear in his eyes that he had forgiven Ben, as if it never happened. They continued walking for a while longer until sunrise. Isaiah found a spot under the shade of a maple tree just to the left of the overgrown train tracks that peeled off to the right. It was out of view. Ben joined Isaiah and sat down, letting out a deep sigh of exhaustion. They rested their heads on the brown crinkled bark and then looked at each other. Their hair pulled from their scalps as they leaned forward, away from the tree. They laughed at each other in embarrassment. Then, with a sigh, they simultaneously settled in for a nap and leaned back into the tree, quickly falling asleep.

After some time, the sound of a roaring train dashing by on the other track jolted the boys awake. Ben rubbed his eyes and stretched into Isaiah's personal space. Isaiah leaned forward but he paused, realizing they had made a foolish mistake picking their spot to sleep.

What is it?" Ben asked.

"My neck and my back are all sticky. My hair is covered in it."

"Great job relaxing at this dumb tree," Ben scoffed.

"Don't act like it was my decision! We both sat here together."

"Shut up. You lured me here."

Isaiah just looked at him. Then, they both started to pull themselves away from the tree leaking sap. They ripped their hair, skin, and shirts in one swift move. Both stood looking up to the moon through the branches and leaves.

"Lured you? How?"

"You were looking all cozy next to the tree, basically begging me to sit next to you." Isaiah stared at him like a cat stares at a dog. "Oh, shut up," Ben said, pushing Isaiah, who didn't seem to move much. With one hand, Isaiah pushed Ben, tossing him onto the train tracks. Ben's back took the impact, and he winced in pain.

"Is that what you wanted?" Isaiah asked, then turned and started walking.

"I guess I deserved that." Ben got up off the ground and caught up to Isaiah. "It's midday; let's go," he said as he took the lead.

Isaiah just smiled at him, then he spun the duffle bag around and unzipped it. He came to a conclusion while shuffling through its contents. "Alright, we've got enough money for another two bus tickets and some cheap food if we can just find a bus station and some type of store," Isaiah said.

"Alright, sounds like a plan."

Isaiah smiled at Ben, "And the plan is we will continue to look for a sign that leads us towards a major city or town. When we know where we are headed, we will catch a bus or train or even grab some food. Whichever comes first. "

"Okay, got it."

The two boys continued their journey, passing under stone bridges and through dark tunnels that ran through mountains. Following the signs, they headed towards Chicago. After reaching a small town, which had a bus headed to Northside Chicago, they walked into a gas station to buy some snacks while they waited. The mini market was completely empty of customers. They walked to the back of the gas station under the watchful eye of the cashier.

"Look at these," Ben said with a mouth-watering tone holding up a plastic bag of sugar covered sour licorice.

"That looks good, and these, too!" Isaiah showed him a bag of cheddar cheese combos.

"Yeah, and these, too," Ben grabbed a bag of potato chips.

"Let's get some drinks, too."

"For sure," Ben agreed. "Definitely need some beverages."

They opened the glass fridge and had cold air blasted into their faces as they looked at the colorful variety of drinks.

"I think we are gonna waste all of the money." Isaiah scratched his head.

"Probably," Ben agreed, laughing as he grabbed a blue sports drink.

"Give me the money! You know what to do, old man!"

Out of nowhere, a man with a mask came into the store; somehow, he did not notice the boys.

"Please, no. I can't keep doing this. I have a family," the cashier cried out as he cowered in fear.

"Does it look like I give a damn?" the masked man growled as he rose a sawed-off shotgun to the cashier's forehead.

"Okay, okay! Please, just don't kill me!" The cashier began to unlock the register.

"Hurry up, old man!" He shot the gun next to him, exploding the cigar wraps into the air behind the register.

"Holy shit what do we do?" Ben whispered to Isaiah, placing their goodies calmly on the floor. They instinctively knew to hide when they heard the yelling and were now crouched behind the shelves. The gas station store had three rows of shelves filled with snacks, cheap apparel, and car oil, with the chilled drinks and alcohol in the back and glass double doors at the front entrance.

"I've got an idea," Isaiah responded.

The man's shouting and the cashier's whimpering covered the sound as Isaiah slowly opened the fridge and very carefully took out two beers from a six-pack case, so as not to make any noise. He quietly closed the fridge.

"Here," Isaiah said softly, handing a beer to Ben.

Then, he whispered a plan in Ben's ear. Ben, with a stern look on his face, nodded his head. Isaiah started sneaking down the left side of the shelf just out of view of the robber, who was to the right in front of the cashier. Ben, on the right side of the shelf, then rolled a beer down the pathway between the shelves and it knocked into the robber's foot. He was stunned, swinging his gun in Ben's direction, who was already hidden again. Then, he turned back to the cashier, who looked even more afraid than before. He knew the gun would be pointed at the kids.

"Don't move!" he commanded the cashier through his muffled mask. Then, he cautiously walked towards where the beer bottle had rolled from, still with the gun pointed towards the cashier. As he reached the end of the aisle, he looked away from the cashier and turned with his gun.

CRASH.

Isaiah creeped behind him and with all his might, swung the beer bottle at the back of his head, shattering it and ripping the back of the mask in the process. Isaiah looked stunned at his own power. Then, Ben pushed over a shelf that fell on top of the masked man, who grunted in pain.

Before running towards the door, the boys grabbed all the snacks off the floor where they left them and tossed the loaded shotgun into the cashier's hands. They dashed out, swinging the glass doors open. The cashier stood in awe, holding the gun in both hands like a tray. After gathering himself, he dialed 911 and aimed the gun at the unconscious masked man.

Ben and Isaiah ran as fast as they could for a while until they saw the bus station. There was a bus arriving as they reached the depot, and they boarded it, pulling out their bag of quarters to hand to the bus driver. The driver smiled and signaled that he needed no additional payment from them. The two boys walked to the back of the bus with bright smiles. Sitting down, they both let out a sigh of relief.

Ben nudged Isaiah, "We just did that."

"Yeah," Isaiah said, staring straight ahead, remembering how hard he hit the robber.

"You saved us man, and we got free food." Ben tried to cheer him up.

Isaiah's mood lightened and he laughed as they began snacking on the cheddar cheese combos, washing each handful down with a swig of their colored sports drinks. They were now farther away from home than they had ever been: the heart of Illinois in the streets of Chicago.

The two boys got off the bus on the north side of Chicago looking for a place to hang out. After walking for some time, they made it downtown. Ben looked up at a low hanging, red, glowing sign in the night sky.

"Gamer Central," Isaiah said, mouth agape, still snacking on the crumbs of combos.

The boys smiled at each other and proceeded inside. They still had money left and decided to hit the arcade area and spend some of it. Still pumped with adrenaline, they were in the moment and weren't thinking ahead. They had never been to an arcade before.

"Let's try that one," Ben exclaimed with a smile.

"Sure, right after I finish these." Isaiah licked his fingers clean of cheese dust and threw out the combo bag.

"Woah, this isn't like anything I've ever tried," said Isaiah, punching the buttons on the arcade game.

"I know. This is crazy. Let's go to that one next!" he suggested, pointing to the robot shooting game.

"Yeah, that looks cool."

The two began playing, discovering that they're pretty good at the game. Eventually, all the money they had was gone. They had used it all to buy tokens, which allowed them to play the games. If they did well, they would receive tickets, and with those tickets, they could buy prizes. On the bright side, they did well. Ben won a pair of jumbo boxing gloves and a basketball. Isaiah won a long, stuffed snake that he coiled around his neck and candy—lots of candy.

"Yo, Zay."

"What's up?"

"Maybe we should stay here."

"How?" Isaiah said as he pulled the plastic wrapper and stuffed another piece of candy into his mouth. They were sitting in a booth at Gamer Central's food court eating their winnings as neon lights flashed around them.

Ben massaged his own temple and looked at the air. "I got it! Let's hide with the laser guns."

"Oh, the laser tag arena. Not a bad idea," Isaiah responded with his mouth full. Ben stared at Isaiah with disgust. "What?" Isaiah asked.

"Shut up."

"Oh, I shouldn't talk while my mouth is full," he said with his mouth full.

"That's true, but no. It's you correcting me for no reason." Ben continued, "When does this place close?"

"I think it's midnight and *there was* a reason."

"How do you even know that? And what reason?"

"There was a sign outside. I was telling you the correct name."

"Shut up, bro. Laser guns or laser tag… it makes no difference. You know what I meant."

The two found a great spot to hide in the laser tag arena and it became their sleeping quarters after closing. In the morning, they would wake and head out into the arcade to challenge kids to competitions, winning their money back on some simple bets. They would then head out for real food outside the arcade. They were dominating the arcade competitions and the staff began to take notice, mostly out of awe. But the manager was becoming wise, noticing that they never seemed to leave and if they did, it was only for a few hours at a time. They left dirt on the carpet, and they smelled like old cheese mixed with their sweaty competitions, bad eating habits, and no hygiene. The boys were just filthy. Pretty soon, all their competitors stopped playing; they were simply unable to bear the stench. The two continued to play, getting even higher scores on just about all the machines. They were addicted and felt like they were unstoppable. The only game the two could never get the hang of was the robot shooting game. There was supposedly an unbreakable record held by the second-biggest slobs there, the Marvin Boys. The Marvin Boys practically owned the machine. While they could never seem to repeat their past greatness, they were still the best at the game.

That is, until Ben and Isaiah began focusing on mastering this game. People left them alone because they smelled but it helped so they could keep practicing with full focus. After only a few days, they began to reach scores the Marvin Boys hadn't in a long time. Children started to watch in fascination, though from a distance. They kept getting better and better. With every play, they recorded a higher score than before. Soon, there was a crowd of people as dense as a dance club on a Friday night. They were all supporting them the whole way, regardless of the boys' stench. Eventually, they used up all their tokens, but not after getting a pile of tickets that flowed from the machine.

"Damn," Ben said, realizing they were out of tokens.

"Yeah," Isaiah agreed.

"Here." A little girl handed the two boys enough tokens for one more round.

"Thanks," Ben and Isaiah said in unison.

"You're welcome...keep going," she responded with a smile and then faded back into the crowd.

"Now, we gotta get it," Ben said to Isaiah as he inserted the tokens into the machine.

"For sure. We're getting the highest score this time."

The little girl backed up and watched in awe as the two boys fixated on the game, immersing themselves into the alternate reality it offered. Everything about the boys switched when they started playing; they got serious. They treated the game as if it were a matter of life or death, giving it their all.

Their hands grew sweaty as they approached the high score. The entire crowd was chanting, "New high score! New high score!" Even some staff members joined in on the fun, though the manager watched on with narrow eyes. The manager walked to each staff member individually, telling them to get back to work. He returned to his office and came up with a brilliant idea. *Check the cameras.*

Isaiah and Ben grew closer and closer to reaching a new high score; the crowd grew loud with them. Then, finally, they did it! After about thirty additional seconds to seal the deal, the boys, exhausted, stopped playing and allowed themselves to lose. They both turned and celebrated with the crowd, screaming in sweet joy. A few people even hugged them, though they instantly regretted it upon entering their personal space, which smelled like rotten eggs and sewage water.

After the crowd dispersed, the previous record holders, the Marvin Boys, emerged and began to walk over.

"So, you think you're tough shit, huh?" yelled out the smaller, scrawny Marvin boy with a squeak in his voice.

"Ha! Look at these losers. They think they're cool 'cause they got a high score on a couple of games. We have the highest scores on all the other games here," spoke the clearly upset taller boy with freckles just under his square glasses. He scrunched his nose and gave a smug look as he spoke.

"What? We don't care. We're just gonna play," Ben said as he turned back around, whipping his now shoulder-length hair around.

"You'll play when we tell you to, punk," the freckled boy threatened.

Ben cleared his throat, "You have the highest scores on all the other games here. The highest score on every game we don't have, right? That's like, what? Fifteen out of the two hundred plus games? The Marvin Boys are a bunch of scrubs."

Benjamin turned away, ending the conversation. The freckled Marvin boy yelled in rage as he swung his fist at the back of Ben's head, sending him to the floor. In an instant, Isaiah turned to the boy, hitting him with a left jab to the forehead, breaking his glasses and sending him to the floor. The scrawny boy saw this and ran screaming.

"I'm sorry! I can't fight, big brother!" he squeaked as he ran.

"I'll remember that," mumbled the freckled boy as he stood and wiped his bloody nose slowly to not cause more pain. He looked at the blood on his hand and then wiped it on his shorts. He assumed a fighting position, ready to attack Isaiah who squared up with him. Just as he leaned forward, ready to pounce, Ben came out of nowhere, hitting the Marvin Boy over the head with his jumbo boxing gloves. The hit sent the kid back to the floor; he laid there screaming in pain, holding his hands over his ear. Ben and Isaiah looked down at him with Ben dropping the gloves on his stomach. The two ran out, not wanting to get caught and having to explain what had just happened.

Some of the staff saw it all go down, but it was fast, and they couldn't be bothered to get involved. The manager walked out of his office, furious just after the boys ran out. In frustration and anger, he called the police and reported the boys for the fight and illegal trespassing. Lucky for Ben and Isaiah, the two cops who arrived saw the whole thing as a joke. They blamed the manager for letting it all happen and not having better security. They said the fight was nothing serious.

Benjamin and Isaiah roamed the rest of the night, unsure of what to do next. They walked for hours and hours, looking at all the places they had never seen in the dense area of Chicago—from the famous Bean to the legendary *L*.

The scrawny Marvin boy told all his friends how these two smelly boys kicked the daylight out of the strongest boy in the local school, his big brother. The Marvin Boys disbanded; the two brothers hated each other after that. Benjamin and Isaiah became legends of the arcade but were banned from ever entering again. It did not matter to the two though because they did not plan on returning anyway. The fun had ended and they were back in the cold and looking for a new place to stay.

After walking for a long time, they ended up in Southside Chicago, just past the *L*, or the elevated rapid transit system, known as the fourth largest transit system in the United States. They arrived at a wide alleyway and saw dry cardboard discarded next to a dumpster and decided this was the best option to sleep for the night. This was an alleyway on the rough side of the city, but it was a bit hidden.

They set their spot up, folding the cardboard into a little house; they weren't pessimistic nor were they optimistic. A door facing the alleyway opened, revealing an old Chinese man with a bucket of rice that was meant to be thrown out. He looked at the boys in pity and slid the bucket over to them across the dark pavement. It bumped a rock and tipped over, spilling some of the rice on the cracked pavement. Benjamin and Isaiah swarmed over it, eating away like ants to a crumb. They felt no shame nor pride; they had not eaten since leaving the arcade a while ago. They devoured it in minutes; after, they looked up to thank the man, but he was already gone.

The man showed up again the next day and the day after that with food for the boys each time. The old man grew attached to the boys, saving food to give to them. They had nowhere to go; the boys would wander the city throughout the day, carefully avoiding authorities to stay out of trouble. When they grew bored or tired, they returned to their cardboard shelter in the alley behind the Chinese restaurant. This became a regular thing for a few weeks, as the old Chinese man became their primary source of food. His pity for them kept them alive.

CHAPTER 13

"You know, this is pretty good," said Ben munching on a leftover shrimp one night.

"Yeah, I'm starting to like the view," Isaiah responded with his hands behind his head as he laid down on their cardboard bed. Ben finished his rice and shrimp, then he laid down next to Isaiah. They looked up at the stars shining down on them and fell asleep, lying against each other like two wild animals. The stars were so bright that night, as if the universe was keeping watch.

The streets were already busy by the time Ben woke up. He got up and yelled to Isaiah who was sitting at the alley's exit. "What's up, Zay? Why didn't you wake me?"

There was no response; he seemed invested in some task at hand, so he approached Isaiah. As he got closer, he saw something in his hands; it was a stray cat.

"Why do you have a—"

Ben was interrupted by the sound of the cat's neck snapping.

"Why did you do that?" Ben yelled.

"I prayed for food and food came." Isaiah looked at Ben with a cold stare.

"What? You fucking psycho."

Isaiah began to explain himself while holding the limp cat by the neck. "I got up early this morning and began praying. I was hungry and the restaurant doesn't always feed us, especially in the morning. So, I prayed for food. Then, I sat down and waited as I continued to pray. Suddenly, this cat came to me and wouldn't leave me alone. I was provided with something to eat."

"What is wrong with you, bro? This god gives you a stray cat for food. You can pray to your god all you want but don't include me."

There was silence. Isaiah stood, still holding the limp cat.

"Zay, you're just weird. How do you even expect to eat it?" Ben snarled.

"I was talking to old Mr. Yu the other day; he said he used to cook cats from time to time when he grew up. So, the restaurant will cook it for me."

"The hell is a matter with you! Nobody is cooking some stray cat in their kitchen."

"So, you don't want any?"

"No, I don't want your dead cat! I want to eat something normal. I thought I was getting used to this. I'm not. This sucks. It's cold and I'm always hungry. It's almost like we left for nothing."

"Don't say that," Isaiah snapped. "We left that place because we had to. There was no other option. And frankly, it was for the best. You'll see. God has a plan for us."

Ben rolled his eyes. "Yeah, yeah. I'm just sick of living in a cardboard box."

"Me too, brother, me too. Now, I'm gonna see if they'll cook this," Isaiah said with a smile. Ben palmed his face.

After a month or so of getting fed by the Chinese restaurant, the two boys decided to find a way to make money and make something out of themselves. They barely existed, had no documentation, no education, and no connections. They tried and tried, applying everywhere they could, but no one was going to hire two smelly, dirty 15-year-old boys without working papers. They stumbled upon a way to make quick money the only way they could: the wrong way. The illegal way.

Isaiah's dark brown skin was flaky from his lack of moisturizing. The dryness he experienced made his ankles and legs look painful. Adding to his cracked skin and addict look was his beaten-up blue jumpsuit and nappy afro, still holding bits of food from the day before.

Benjamin had a terrible stench and moppy hair that clumped together. His face was dirty, and his neck had a terrible rash on it. He wore a dingy white cartoon t-shirt and a black zip up sweatshirt. His bottoms were ripped up jeans that were a little too small for him and showed his ankles.

They met the self-proclaimed king of the streets after an altercation with a group of his runners. There were drug runners everywhere—business everywhere. There were specific corners for specific people and important clients all over. Messing with this system meant messing with the streets. Fate guided them towards The Throne.

After one boy had mistakenly dropped some of the drugs out of his backpack, Isaiah picked it up. The boy did not know what he had lost until he made it to his destination.

"Akkun, you got the stuff?"

"Yessir, right here." An Asian-American boy with curly brown hair rummaged through his bag until his face began to sink and his heart dropped. The man he was delivering the drugs to was large and strong; he looked like a linebacker. The heavy man grabbed him by the shirt and pulled him close.

"You better find that shit or else nobody will find you," he whispered in his ear.

Akkun backed up, terrified, nodded his head to show he understood, and then turned and ran back the way he came, praying to God he could find what he had lost.

Looking at it in the sunlight, Isaiah tried to identify what it was. He held it up in the air, pondering the possibilities.

Sniff. "It kinda smells like skunk," Ben said, trying to help Isaiah realize what it was.

"Hey, actually this might be—"

Out of nowhere, Isaiah was tackled to the ground by Akkun, who was accompanied by a few other young runners. An all-out brawl was let loose between Ben, Isaiah, and three young drug runners. Ben ripped Akkun off Isaiah and began to swing his arms viciously at his head as they fell to the floor. In the meantime, the other two runners took on Isaiah. As they surrounded him, Isaiah took a defensive stance. One runner swung at him; he dodged the punch and grabbed his arm, throwing him into the other runner. Then, he grabbed Ben, pulling him off an already beaten Akkun and left them in a bloody mess.

After hearing of this news, the self-proclaimed king of the streets dispersed more runners through the Southside in search of them. However, Ben and Isaiah outwitted him Upon realizing they were being hunted, the two boys didn't return to their cardboard shelter. Instead, they took to the rooftops and tried to find out who was controlling all these minions.

On the rooftop of one of the buildings, they dropped the drugs they still had in their possession and then climbed down into the one-way alleyway. After some time, one of the drug runners came into the alleyway and Isaiah and Ben appeared in front of him, ready to punch and kick, asking questions later. Before they could attack, the boy raised his hands in fear while holding a note.

"What's that?"

"This is from The Throne. He wants to see you."

Ben slowly took the paper from his sweaty grasp and then backed up. He tried to read it out loud. "To you. Two young. Um…" He stuttered. "Here, you read it," he said, handing the paper to Isaiah.

Isaiah read the following out loud. "To the two young bucks, you've started trouble for me by taking my drugs and attacking my boys. But after hearing of your skills, I'm willing to make you an offer. Meet me underneath the I-90 overpass, by the parking lot. Tonight, at eleven."

"I-90? That's near Chinatown, right?" Ben jolted.

"Yeah, you're right," Isaiah affirmed.

The boy who delivered the note tried to leave, but he was stopped by Isaiah's muscular arm, which was blocking his way. Isaiah gave a sinister stare, then let him go.

"So, do you think we should go?" Benjamin asked.

CHAPTER 14

"Do you *want* to go?" Isaiah asked.

"Yeah, why not?" Ben responded.

"Because it's a set-up. What do you think they are going to do? Do you really think we'll be welcomed with open arms right after we beat up some of them?"

"But Isaiah, the note said we had skills. He wants to use our skills."

"Sure, let's say the leader doesn't kill us and takes us in instead. We will be just like those punks we beat up, running drugs and being used."

"So what? They do it for a reason, right? There's a lot of money that comes with the risk. Am I wrong?"

"No, you're right."

"We should do it. Save the money and go get a place for ourselves. Just the two of us. Then we can find some legal stuff to do."

Isaiah was silent, scratching his head and thinking over the situation.

"Bro, do you want to stay in the alley eating people's trash? Or do you want to get out here and do something with our lives?"

Again, there was a long silence as Isaiah thought it over.

"Ben, it doesn't matter how I look at it; this is a very bad idea. We will most certainly run into trouble, and we'll be risking our lives. This isn't a 'let's try it out' kind of scenario. If you're wrong, we may die."

"I know, I know, but Zay, I'm not stupid, okay? What other choice do we have?"

"You know what, fine. Wherever you go, I will follow. Still, this is a terrible idea, even if it works out. I got a gut feeling about it."

"It'll be alright. Just trust me."

"I'm going to pray before we go." Isaiah turned to the wall and knelt. He slowly folded his hands and brought them to his head as he bowed with closed eyes.

Ben shook his head and rolled his eyes. After ten seconds, he started tapping his foot and couldn't wait any longer. He wanted to meet the new world that waited for them. "Done yet?" Ben pushed Isaiah.

Isaiah opened his eyes and smiled at Ben. " Yep, all done. Let's go."

It was nightfall and the boys were just arriving at the agreed upon destination. "This area looks pretty nice," Ben said, scanning the area.

"Nice? In what way?" Isaiah countered.

"I don't know. It's just cool being underneath all the moving cars." Ben looked up; his sunken eyes seemed to be making a revival.

The two were waiting for Tyrone underneath the I-90 overpass, just like the note said. It was dark now and there was little to no light illuminating the overpass. They heard nothing but their own voices and the cars whizzing by.

"Did you hear that?"

"No, what?"

"Shh." Isaiah motioned his finger to Ben.

"Don't tell me to shush." Ben slapped his finger away.

The two boys walked slower than before, adrenaline secreting through their bodies. They started breathing heavily; with each step, their bodies became more tense. They did not know what was waiting for them, but they smelled bloodlust in the air. Isaiah looked angry, pissed off even. Ben was frantically looking around, reacting to every sound he heard like a scared rat. They were concerned for their lives with each breath they took, trying not to exhale too loud. As they tried to control their breathing, Ben felt his legs tremble. Isaiah guided him forward, encouraging him to walk on courageously.

The night was cold and dark with an ominous feel to it. They walked into an empty parking lot underneath the overpass. One flickering streetlamp covered the lot with light. The two boys stood underneath the light, staring up at it. The light stopped flickering and stayed on. The brightness revealed men hunched over, hiding in the corners of the parking lot.

Isaiah and Ben were too shocked to react; they just stared at the men as they slowly stood and walked towards them from across the lot. It seemed as if an army were pouring out into the lot. The streetlamp flickered once more and went out, leaving them in utter darkness. The group of men sprinted at the boys with an onslaught of kicks and punches. Ben and Isaiah, who tried their best to defend themselves in the dark of the night, immediately starting to swing back. One of the men had a bat. After Isaiah punched one of them with an uppercut, the bat met the back of his head. He fell unconscious to the ground and was immediately bombarded with kicks in his face and stomach as he laid there, motionless.

Ben had fallen but got back up, still trying to fight back. The men focused on Ben, and he fell back down, beating him with kicks and punches. The man with the bat got a few swings in his gut before Ben fell unconscious, as well. One man kicked Ben in the teeth for good measure. The group laughed and then disappeared in the night as fast as they had appeared. With no cameras or witnesses, the boys received no help. Not that they expected any.

"That's some scary shit," one of the men who was just standing and watching said.

"No kidding, Frank," another agreed. "Give me a light, will ya?"

"No problem, Art." They smoked their cigarettes as they watched the two boys suffer.

Tyrone looked on with no emotion in his eyes while smoking a blunt. "I love this shit," he smiled.

"Yeah, you're fucked up, Throne." Both Frank and Art laughed with Tyrone until Ben and Isaiah were completely unconscious, wheezing with every breath.

"Alright, that's enough. Time to head home," Tyrone announced.

With that, everyone scattered and left Isaiah and Ben alone, bleeding out in the empty lot.

Isaiah woke up first, coughing into the dirt, sucking dust in, and coughing some more. Isaiah's head was covered in blood and his nose was clearly broken. He could barely move but managed to roll over slowly, wincing in pain as he rested his hand on Benjamin's.

Ben woke up slowly, blinking several times before being able to keep his eyes open. He saw Isaiah's hand on his and placed his opposite hand onto Isaiah's.

"Did we win?" Ben asked with a smile.

Isaiah started laughing and then started coughing again, in serious pain. "Don't make me laugh man."

"Sorry. I don't regret it though."

"Making me laugh?"

"No, dummy, I don't regret coming here."

Isaiah looked away and took a deep breath. There was a long silence as they laid there together in the dirt and blood.

"Thanks for sticking it out with me. You're my brother for real. My family for life," Benjamin said.

"I promised that I'd never leave you. You've got a long life ahead of you."

"We both do, together," Ben said. They smiled and laid their heads back down in the dirt.

The two boys took a long time to get up. Finally, they mustered the strength to walk back to their alleyway, limping along the way, covered in blood. Surprisingly, nobody asked them what had happened, and nobody stopped to see if they needed help.

That is, until they approached their alley and their cardboard home. A black SUV pulled up next to them and rolled down the passenger seat window. It revealed a dark-skinned man with black shades on. "Get in," he commanded with a deep voice.

"What?" Ben was so confused.

"No." Isaiah tried to walk away, pulling Ben by his hand.

"Wasn't asking."

The back door opened and a large man got out. He picked up the young boys and tossed them in the van like they were groceries.

"Assholes!" Ben yelled in frustration.

"Say that again," the large man dared.

Ben spat at him instead. The man slapped Ben in response, almost sending him unconscious again. Ben leaned side to side as blood and saliva leaked from his mouth. Isaiah was silent as he watched, his eyes resembling that of a wild animal waiting for the opportunity to pounce. His stone-cold stare spooked the large man a bit. The large man sat in the back with them, while two other men sat in the front.

"Yo Art, are we good?" the man in the passenger seat said.

116

Art, the large man, leaned in view of the rearview mirror and nodded.

They all remained silent as the car drove around the city of Chicago. Isaiah realized there was nothing he could do except care for Ben. After some time, Ben was fully conscious with a piercing headache. The man in the passenger seat had dark shades on with expensive jewelry that chimed together as he moved. He watched the boys closely.

"The drugs you took. Those were mine. The routes you fucked up, that's my problem. You paid your price. I can see my dogs did a good job on you young bucks." He started laughing. His voice was so deep Ben thought his head was vibrating.

"Listen, over here…around these parts, they call me The Throne. I run these streets. I'm the king of it all. So now, like I wrote on that little note, I recognize y'all got heart. That's what I need out here. I want you two running for me, now. We got eyes and spies; we know you got nowhere to go." The Throne turned around in his seat and faced them.

"I can give you a home. I can give you a family. Join my gang and take the right of passage."

The car continued to drive around; they were all silent for a while.

Breaking the silence, Isaiah spoke first, "What if we don't want to join your gang?"

"What? You're gonna." Throne had a ghastly smile.

"Or what?" Ben asked.

"*Or what?*" He laughed with thunder yet again. "Or how about I blow your brains out right now? Huh?" Throne said, flexing a 9 mm. "Man, y'all be funny. Aight, I'll see you soon," Throne glared.

Art tossed the two boys from the black SUV onto the dirty sidewalk by their alleyway.

"You won't find us again," Ben yelled.

"I have eyes everywhere, boy. I'm always watching." Throne smiled that ghastly smile yet again. He put the window up and the car drove away.

Ben and Isaiah limped back to the alley and onto their cardboard bed. Exhausted and worn out, all they wanted was to fall asleep. Their minds raced and they stared at the dark sky. Ben looked ready to cry. Isaiah feared for him and asked God what he should do next but he was given no response. Ben drowned in fear of what the future held in store for them.

In the middle of the night, Isaiah rubbed his eyes and looked around.

"Still dark out," he mumbled to himself before deciding to go back to sleep. But as he laid back down, Isaiah felt Ben twitch. So, he sat back up and watched Ben, though it was hard to see. He twitched again, yet more aggressively this time. Isaiah heard him whimper and saw the outline of his face, which resembled a frown. Ben started shaking in fear while still asleep. Isaiah teared up and laid down closer to him. He held him tight and whispered into his ear, "It's okay Ben. I'm here." Isaiah embraced Ben as he violently shook, still asleep, trapped inside his own mind. "Everything is going to be alright. We can handle it," He repeated. "We can handle it."

The morning sunrise peaked itself into the alleyway and woke Isaiah. Isaiah woke Ben and they slowly got up, each of them smelling like sewage and looking even worse. The two boys laid back down and rested for a while. At about midday, they decided to get up, limping through the streets. They walked side-by-side, clearly too young to be wandering the streets during the school day. Lots of people stared but the boys were more invested in their conversation to care.

"Really? You don't think God has a plan for you?" Isaiah was skeptical of Ben's statement.

"Yeah, no. Like, what plan? What plan does this "good" god of yours have for shitty old me? Look at me. Look at us! Bro, c'mon. That's a fairytale."

"You just can't come to accept that the pain you feel from losing your family was meant to strengthen you, can you? Your father was a good man, and you are, too. Stop playing the victim."

Ben was too stunned to speak at first. "The fuck did you just say?" Ben pushed Isaiah but he barely moved. Again, he pushed him, but this time, with all his strength. Isaiah leaned over and stumbled a bit. Then, in one motion, he adjusted his footing, grabbed Isaiah by the arm, and tossed him over his shoulder. Ben landed on a trash can, which gave some buffer before hitting the concrete.

"Asshole!" Ben yelled as he struggled to get up.

"I barely touched you."

Ben finally got to his feet and rushed to Isaiah. Isaiah stood his ground and pushed Ben back. Ben began to swing at Isaiah, though he effortlessly dodged them all. Some onlookers saw the scuffle and raised a commotion. Before they realized, the authorities were on their way, their sirens trumpeting just a couple blocks away. Reluctantly, Ben stopped fighting; he and Isaiah ran from the scene and continued walking for hours. They had forgotten about their injuries, yet they were still limping.

It was starting to get dark, and they were near the *L*. Specifically, the boys were approaching the loop. Their plan was to walk into the train loop and wait for Tyrone at Millennium Park.

"He should find us here if he's looking," Ben said and Isaiah nodded in agreement. Sooner than later, the black SUV pulled up nearby and honked. Ben and Isaiah made their way over to it.

"So, you guys are in, right?"

Ben looked at Isaiah and then looked back. "Yeah, we're in."

"Now, that's what we like to hear. Hop in." The SUV's door swung open, and they climbed into the back seat.

CHAPTER 15

The initiation began that night, led by Tyrone, the self-proclaimed king of the streets or The Throne, and the leader of the 21 Dragons. Throne gathered his gang members at a local park. There were about ten cars with music blasting, with the 21 Dragon members standing around smoking blunts and drinking 40s. Throne stood on a rock and raised his hands. Someone instantly turned the music down and the talking ceased. They all looked at The Throne, waiting for what was to be announced.

"Today, we make a toast. For these two." Throne pulled Ben and Isaiah to his side. Then, he lifted his Styrofoam cup. "Our newest and youngest 21 Dragons."

All the members lifted their blunt or drink and gave a nod to the two young boys. They all whooped in agreement.

"According to tradition, there must be a beating into submission before being able to enter the gang. These two young bulls managed to get their asses whooped so bad, ol' Ben over here's still limping from it. I'm willing to make an exception for you two, seeing it's already been done. It's only right."

Again, the gang members shouted in agreement. Ben and Isaiah pledged to not reveal any information if caught or lead police to the safe house. The gang was to be a tight knit group that fought for each other. Ben and Isaiah were the youngest members of 21 Dragons.

"I will finish the initiation with them tonight." With that, the gang was dismissed. Little by little, they left the park until only Frank, Art, Throne, Ben, and Isaiah were left.

"What do you mean *finish*?" Ben asked.

"You gotta wear the mark." Each member wore a tattoo of a dragon on their right wrist, which meant they would have to, as well. Part of the initiation into the gang required them to receive the tattoo and wear it as a badge of honor.

They left the park and drove downtown, where they were escorted to a dingy and dark basement. A large man full of tattoos and thirty or so piercings sat waiting for them. He had a raspy voice and the same tattoo of a dragon as the gang members on his right wrist.

"Is it gonna hurt?" Ben asked.

"Only if you're a little chica. Just hop on the seat, gringo."

"Don't call me a gringo. Don't call me a chica either," Ben puffed.

"Okay, okay, my friend, I will call you nothing."

"Thank you."

"Now, come, sit."

"Isaiah, you go first," Ben turned.

Isaiah rolled his eyes and stepped onto the seat. He leaned back and relaxed.

After about thirty minutes, it was done. The area was cleaned and wrapped with an adhesive film to heal.

"How was it?" Ben asked as Isaiah sat up.

"I don't know. I think I fell asleep."

Throne started laughing.

"This one's crazy, bro," the tattoo artist chuckled.

"I know; he's different," Throne responded.

"Your turn." The artist looked at Ben.

Ben grimaced and got onto the seat but could not relax at all.

"Stay still or else this won't go well."

"I'm trying."

"Don't look at it; think of something else."

Ben looked away and began to study the walls of the basement instead. It actually helped; the needle wasn't bothering him as much. But still, every few minutes, he would wince in pain.

"All done. See, that wasn't so bad."

"Sure, but it wasn't so good either," Ben snapped.

"Hey, I did a good job."

"Not the tattoo. The pain. Maybe the tattoo is okay," Ben said as he admired the work and hopped off the seat. He took his place next to Isaiah.

The artist stood and looked at The Throne. "A este hombre blanco le van a golpear el,[1]" the artist said to Throne.

"Conozco a mi amigo; realmente lo pide. No sé qué voy a hacer con él, pero su gran amigo aquí es muy útil,[2]" Throne responded.

"Parece servicial, un hombre de aspecto fuerte. Freak de la naturaleza casi. De todos modos, nos vemos pronto. Mantente a salvo mi amigo, avísame si me necesitas,[3]" the artist said as he shook The Throne's hand.

"Lo haré mi amigo, estaré en contacto,[4]" Throne responded, then he turned and walked up the stairs with the two boys following him. They went outside to the black SUV where Art was in the driver's seat,

---

[1] "This white kid is asking to get hit."

[2] "I know my friend, he really asks for it. I don't know what I'm going to do with him. His best friend here though, he is very useful."

[3] "He seems like he'd be useful. Strong looking kid, freak of nature almost. Anyway, see you soon. Stay safe my friend and let me know iof you need anything."

[4] "I will my friend, I will stay in touch."

waiting. His eyes were wide open, scanning his surroundings. Ben, Isaiah, and The Throne got into the car.

"Aight, let's go, Art." Art pulled away.

"Now that y'all in the gang for real, it's time to show you how things are done."

They stood in a junkyard, where Frank and Art had set up targets with liquor bottles in varying distances and heights. Throne began to talk with Ben and Isaiah as he pulled on a reefer, smoke billowing in between his words.

"Ya know, Frank grew up in Northside, Chicago. He used to be a security guard for celebrities before returning to the streets. He used to know my cousin, Reed, may he rest in peace." Throne pounded his chest, kissed his knuckle, and pointed to the sky. "His old gang is all but gone or retired, so he came to me. Arthur never left the streets. He knew me when I was just Tyrone. Arthur's the oldest guy we got; he's like in his fifties or sixties or something. They taught me a lot; they gon' teach both of you, too."

"Here, kid, take this," Art said, handing Ben a glock .40.

"This one suits you." Art gave Isaiah a .38 Smith & Wesson.

"Now, aim using these things that poke out; they're called sights. You only have a back sight on that one, Isaiah. But what you want to do is line up the front of the gun with the back sight and aim at the bottle."

They both began to aim. Ben was ready to shoot.

"Hang on, kid. Be careful with it. This one doesn't have a safety. Get used to aiming first. Don't hold it so close; stretch your arms out a bit. Good job, Isaiah. That's it."

They aimed for a while. After Art determined they were comfortable enough, he showed them how to turn the safety off and on. They both aimed and looked ready.

"We'll take turns. Ben, you go first, then Isaiah, until you're all out of bullets."

Ben looked through his front sight and lined it up with the back sight. His arms were out but still bent, and he held the gun still. He took his first shot as he aggressively pulled the trigger. The bullet raced out of the gun and whizzed by the bottle, hitting a wrecked car behind it.

"That wasn't bad," Art said, but Ben scoffed at the remark.

Isaiah shot with no hesitation and popped one of the liquor bottles, sending glass in every direction.

"Hey! There we go!" Art jumped and turned to Isaiah.

Ben rolled his eyes as Throne, Art, and Frank commended him. Ben waited for them to back up and took his time aiming again. Again, he missed. Isaiah fired immediately after, and he hit another bottle. He was congratulated yet again.

Ben went to shoot again, making sure he was perfectly lined up. He took a deep breath and as he breathed out, he shot. This time, it was nowhere close, hitting a trash pile off to the left. In his frustration, Ben yelled and began firing uncontrollably at all the bottles that were lined up. He fired five times before the magazine ran out. Not one bullet met the target. Ben threw the gun to the floor.

"Stupid gun. The thing's broken."

Isaiah turned the safety on and handed his gun back to Art. Meanwhile, Throne picked up the gun Ben threw to the ground, brushing the dirt off.

"Yo, Frank, toss me a mag." Frank threw a magazine to Throne. He caught it and loaded it into the gun in one motion. He aimed just as Ben had, fired, and hit a bottle. Then, he did it one-handed. Again, he hit a bottle. Side armed, upside down, eyes closed—you name it. Every shot hit its target until there were no bottles left.

"I think it works fine." They all smirked as they walked back to the car, except Ben. Ben was in absolute awe.

Ben and Isaiah had agreed to become Throne's "go-to" runners, mostly because they had nothing else to do. They began to run drugs throughout Chicago for the summer while still sleeping on cardboard. They didn't mind sleeping outside until winter arrived.

One of the gang members they had taken a liking to was O-time. They never bothered to learn his real name because everyone just called him O-time. He was calm and easy to hang out with, hated to argue, and loved to eat. O-time's house was where the important business meetings went down. So, he was mostly at home, eating. His family knew he was in the gang and didn't care much. They just asked that everyone follow the house rules. Just a few, simple rules. No fighting in the house. No girls in the house. No feet on the sofas.

One night after the gang was finished smoking in O-time's house, they began to go their separate ways. Ben and Isaiah stayed until everyone had left, almost waiting to be kicked out. Ben was building up the courage to go out into this particularly frigid night. Isaiah waited for Ben. Thankfully, O-time realized the situation and was nice enough to offer them a place to stay. O-time never asked for anything in return. as long as they followed the house rules.

Ben and Isaiah were thankful and did just that. The two boys were heavily involved with two of the main gang members, Frank and Art. Even during the winter days, when the snow was up to their hips, Isaiah and Ben made drug runs by their command. They would receive bags of marijuana or cocaine from Frank or Art, and sometimes Throne himself. They would put the plastic bags in their socks. Depending on the load, they sometimes used a book bag, taking it to a certain location or directly to whoever requested it. They would collect payment, drop off the package, and return the money. The dealers would give them a cut of the profit. This is how they made their money, allowing them to afford clothes from goodwill, snacks, shoes, and other necessities. The boys stunk and rarely bathed but occasionally, O-Time allowed them to shower at the house. O-Time never asked for anything in return, just that everyone respect the house rules.

Both Ben and Isaiah were thankful that things seemed to have turned around for them. They were comfortable in the city and the daily routine. But Ben had begun developing a new focus. One that only included him. Isaiah didn't seem as important anymore. Ben envied The Throne and wanted to claim the kingdom as his own. He planned to make a name for himself, and eventually make it big. Isaiah and Ben had stopped sleeping next to each other. They began to drift apart as Ben pursued things Isaiah wasn't concerned with.

Isaiah was just there because Ben was; he did not like it in the least. He did the jobs asked of him and did them well, without complaint. His only focus was making sure Ben was okay. Over time, Isaiah grew silent; he barely spoke to Ben, let alone anyone else. He grew taller and his shoulders were broader than before. Isaiah scared people that walked past him, although it was not his intent. It was just that his presence was so commanding and powerful. He stood far above everyone else in strength and height. As time moved on, Ben grew, as well. It seemed to him that he could never catch up to his brother, so he stopped training and focused on his reputation, not realizing he would regret this decision later on.

CHAPTER 16

It had been a year since the two boys joined the gang. They were now well-known as a part of the 21 Dragons and had the tattoos to prove it. Benjamin relished the fact that they no longer slept in a dirty alley nor did they survive on scraps. They now ate well and had a real place to sleep. Even though it wasn't their own, they felt welcomed at O-Time's house.

Throne had purchased a building with plans to eventually make it a weightlifting gym, but for now, it was a safe house for storage and safety. Throne told Ben and Isaiah that they would be able to sleep in the back room when everything was set up and ready. Benjamin felt they were moving up and accepted the offer for them both. He began helping to set up the gym. Throne was selling monthly memberships for fifteen dollars per month, and Ben and Isaiah were free to work out whenever they pleased. Isaiah made great use of his free membership, working out every morning. Ben hit the weights sometimes, but he didn't have the dedication. Plus, he was focused on making progress with his reputation in the streets. Throne planned to buy more buildings and create a bigger business to grow his influence and fronts for money laundering.

The core of the 21 Dragons gang all sat on O-Time's couch smoking a joint with Ben and Isaiah.

"Finally!" Throne jolted from his seat.

"What? What is it?"

"My dawg, Z. He's out of prison today."

"Z? I've never heard you talk about anyone named Z," said one of the members.

"Nothing to say. Man was locked up."

"What's he like?" Ben was clearly interested.

"Oh, Z and I go way back!" Throne said with a slow smile. "That man saved my life countless times. In fact, Z was in jail for that exact reason, giving a shooter the work before he could get me. Forever in debt to Z. He's been away for like fifteen years now."

"Sounds like a legend to get you going like this," Mikey smiled.

"Damn straight. I'm about to go pick him up now. Frank, you coming?" Frank got up and began to follow Throne out.

"Can I come?" Ben asked with a raised eyebrow.

"Uh. Yeah, sure, why not? Come meet Z, little man."

As Frank drove them in the black SUV to pick up Z from prison, Ben noticed that he had no weapon, even though Throne, Arthur, and Frank were strapped with their pistols. Even if it was a trip to pick up rolling paper, or simply get some food, they were never without their guns. Today was no different; both Frank and The Throne were ready for anything. They arrived at the prison and waited for Z to come out.

"Damn, that motherfucker got huge!" Throne laughed.

"He's a big boy," Frank added.

"Yo, Z, we over here," Throne yelled to the muscular man.

Z walked over to them. Throne and Frank got out of the car to greet him, and Ben followed suit.

"How you been, Z?" Throne asked as he gave him a hug, pounding his back.

"Better now, that's for sure." He dapped up Frank and then looked at Benjamin. "Who's the shrimp?"

"I ain't a shrimp!" Ben immediately reacted.

"Chill out, little man." Z looked at Throne for explanation.

"This is Ben." Throne stood behind Ben and placed his hands on his shoulders. "This kid is gonna learn from you."

"Like hell! Why should I teach this shrimp anything?"

"I'm not a damn shrimp!" Ben interrupted.

Z lightly shoved Ben and he fell into the car door, then awkwardly landed on the ground. Frank tried to help him up, but Ben slapped his hand away.

"Chill out, Z. Not the car," Throne reacted.

"Who does this kid think he is?" Z ignored Throne. Ben looked up at Z from the ground with the eyes of a killer. "A wild one huh?"

"For certain," Throne added. "He thinks he can run this gang someday. Cocky kid, but I like his grit." Throne got more honest. "Plus, his almost inseparable friend is built like a linebacker."

"Wow, I guess I'll see for myself. Huh, shrimp?" Ben was silent as rage built inside him. "That's right, little shrimp. Get angry. Use that fuel for wherever you're headed."

Ben had just met him, but he already hated Z. It was hard to understand the respect the self-proclaimed king of the streets showed Z. Ben now found a new purpose, one that was far easier for him. Instead of trying to prove himself, he needed to become like Z and make people recognize his worth. This man, whom the old streets respected, and the new streets would be forced to, demanded acknowledgment without asking. If Ben could be just like Z, then he would command the respect.

"Let's take you home, Z," Throne said.

They got back into the SUV. When Z was arrested at thirteen years old, he still lived with his mother, so that's where they were headed. On the way, they passed a basketball court and Z demanded that they stop.

"What? What is it?" Frank asked.

"Just wait here a minute. I haven't played at my home court in far too long."

Throne got out of the car with Z and began to laugh. "Come on, man. You're trash. You ain't nice no more."

They stopped at a rectangular concrete court with two elevated horizontal hoops with open nets hanging on each side of the court. It was covered on every side with a fifteen-foot wire fence. The hoops were the goals; their poles which held them above ground were cemented into the concrete. The hoops or the rims were oversized and welded to the backboard so as not to be stolen.

"Where are we?" Ben asked Frank, still inside the car.

"Z's old playground, the basketball court. I remember this young delinquent used to play kids one-on-one for their lunch money. A boy with a talent that never cared much about the sport. Just had fun giving someone a bucket." Frank laughed until he began to cough. As Frank struggled to catch his breath, Ben tried to imagine what a young Z would look like.

Z picked up a weathered and waterlogged basketball. He passed it to Throne who had made his way onto the court with him.

"Damn, this shit's heavy."

Throne shot the ball and air balled, missing the net, rim, and backboard altogether. Ben had gotten out of the SUV and was watching intently from behind the fence. Z laughed as Throne bowed his head. This had stunned Ben—to see the self-proclaimed king of the streets humbled.

"'Man, see, you're trash, not me," Z said.

"Chill, man. That ball is trash," Throne defended himself.

Z picked up the waterlogged ball and tried to dribble it. It barely bounced and water sprayed when it did. Still, Z pounded the ball even harder until it came up to his waist. Even with baggy clothes on, Benjamin could see the monstrous muscles rippling beneath. Z backed up far deeper than Throne and shot the ball behind the long half circle shaped 3-point line. The ball spun in the air until it landed straight through the rim while barely touching the net.

"Damn." Throne was surprised. "So, you still got it?"

"Never lost it. Best believe I was killing them in the pound."

"Y'all wanna play some two on twos? Ones and twos?" A tall light skinned boy walked up to them holding his own ball under his arm. No one noticed him until he entered the court, which is surprising, considering he stood at six foot and nine inches with dyed blonde hair and earrings. He was skinny but had a muscular and athletic frame.

"Twos? Us two verses you and who?" Throne asked.

"How about that little white kid? He looks like he could use a friend," the tall boy asked as he pointed to Ben sitting on the grass behind the fence. Throne laughed and shook his head.

Z spoke up, disregarding Throne. "Yeah, take him. Three pointers are two points and layups or close shots are one point"

"Bet. Yo, white boy! Come over here!" Ben pointed at himself, surprised. "Yes you. Come here," the tall boy yelled, motioning Ben over with his arms.

Ben got up slowly, confused as he walked over to the entrance. He walked even slower and with his head down as he made his way over to the tall boy. Ben said with a crack in his voice, "What's up?" He stared up at the giant before himself.

"You're on my team," the tall skinny giant said to him.

"Uh, okay." Ben smiled, though he felt nervous.

"What's your name?" the tall kid asked.

"Ben. What about you?"

"Raymond, but most people just call me RJ."

"RJ, cool."

"Yeah, cool."

They laughed and turned to Z and The Throne, who were waiting patiently to begin the game.

"I'll shoot for it." Z shot the waterlogged ball and made the shot.

"Good shot, Z," Throne commended.

"Your ball, but we're using mine." RJ handed his ball to Z; it wasn't brand new, but the rounded synthetic rubber layer had a worn in grip, which Z liked.

"Ah, much better." He tossed the water filled ball aside and let Throne have a look.

"Check up, let's start the game."

RJ guarded Z and Ben guarded The Throne. Ben had seen basketball played on TV before and played a little in gym class while in middle school.

Z passed the ball to RJ, who passed it back, signaling the start of the game. Z passed the ball to Throne, while Ben did his best to guard him. Throne began dribbling the ball with force, sizing Ben up. In an instant, Throne raced to the hoop. Ben tried his best to stop his path, but Throne leaned his shoulder into Ben, causing Ben to fall back and land on the concrete. Throne took the open path to the hoop and laid it through the net.

"One to zero." Throne laughed and mocked Ben.

RJ walked over and helped Ben up, "Don't worry about it."

"Game to eleven," Z said as he checked the ball. Once Z had the ball, he scored by running through Ben.

"Damn, I didn't know you were this soft, kid," Throne laughed as he flexed on Ben. It happened four more times until Ben finally had enough. He snarled and dug deep into the rage that was beginning to grow inside him.

Being far more aggressive and intense, Ben stayed in front of Throne and didn't let him dribble. When he tried to, Ben would slap the ball away. After Ben slapped the ball twice, the third time, he missed. As he reached in, Throne spun around him and again scored an easy shot right at the rim.

"Seven to zero. You two are about to get shut out." Throne smiled as he checked the ball to Ben.

"Seven to zero; we got this, Ben. C'mon." RJ patted him on the back and gave him a high five.

It was rare for someone to not give up on Ben after seeing him fail so many times in a row. RJ seemed different, like Isaiah. Supportive and forgiving. Ben's frown turned into a smile and then an intoxicating energy oozed out of him like he was filled with some spirit.

Z saw this in Ben's expression and was taken aback. Still, he passed the ball to Throne, curious as to what might happen. Throne sensed no threat from Ben, even with this new sense of motivation. Ben gave it his all, staying in front of him and making every single dribble difficult. He constantly pressured Throne and almost stole it on a few attempts. Throne broke through his defense yet again and took two steps to the hoop. Ben ran with him, tearing at the ball, but ultimately, Throne powered through again and got the shot off into the air.

To Throne's surprise, RJ was waiting for it. He met the ball midair and spiked it to the ground. It bounced so hard it went over the fence. RJ said nothing but went to retrieve the ball.

Z gave Throne a look with his eyebrow raised. Throne raised his shoulders in confusion.

"Homie high key got up."

"For real," Z agreed.

RJ returned the ball and checked it up. Throne was still thinking about the previous play as RJ carelessly passed the ball to Throne, who was covered by Ben, still burning with the desire to win. Ben stole the pass and gave it to RJ, who immediately dribbled to the hoop. With an open lane, he took off the ground and slammed the ball through the hoop with two hands. He swung on the rim with his legs bent as he roared out.

After returning to the ground, he gave Ben a high five and checked the ball up. He gave it to Ben and Ben gave it back. RJ dribbled past the outside line towards the hoop. As Z backed up to stop him, RJ snatched the ball between his legs and stepped back, creating a separation of ten feet or so. Then, he shot the ball wide open, and it swished through the net.

"Six to two, check up."

"It's seven to three," Throne corrected.

"Same shit, bro."

Ben was stunned. Did RJ even know who he was talking to? It didn't seem to matter; his mind was on the game.

They continued to score as RJ did it all himself—majestic dribble moves that led into beautiful shots or crazy quick drives to the hoop followed by powerful dunks on top of both Throne and Z. Ben stayed at the three-point line, simply passing the ball to RJ each time. He stood there dumbfounded, in complete shock as to how RJ consistently nailed it.

By the time he missed a shot, the score was seven to nine. They got the ball and Z hit a close shot.

"So, what's the score now?"

"We're up, nine to eight," Ben said with a smile.

"What are you smiling at, boy? You ain't done shit but watch," Throne said to Ben.

Who're you calling boy? RJ just made you look like a toddler. What kinda throne are you sitting on? is what Ben wanted to say. "Scoreboard," is what Ben actually said.

"Watch how you talk to me before I make this little game real life." Throne was mad and getting madder.

"Y'all street dudes are really crazy. Who gets this mad about a game?" RJ said without an ounce of fear.

Ben was inspired by his blind bravery, and Throne knew RJ didn't know any better. Throne let RJ's disrespect slide and continued the game.

"It doesn't matter. Cause the game is about to be over," Z said, commanding the attention to himself.

"Oh, is it now? Let's see." RJ smiled and checked the ball up. Z hit two-point shots in back to back possessions and ended the game.

"We have seen," Z said as he made the final shot. "That's game over."

"Good game. You're a pretty good hooper. Did you play anywhere?" RJ asked Z and then took a sip from his water bottle.

"The yards." Z and Throne began to laugh together. "Nah, I ain't never play anywhere for real."

"Well, you're pretty good."

"Yeah, I know," Z smiled. "You're not too bad yourself. Keep at it and you could be something someday. How old are you? Nineteen? Twenty-two?"

"Seventeen."

"Damn! Seventeen?! How in the hell are you built like that at seventeen? Lord have mercy on your body, and you'll go far, my boy. You playing at the high school?"

"Appreciate it, man. Yeah, one of the local schools. I gotta go but it was nice meeting y'all." RJ gave them a fist bump and walked towards Ben to say goodbye.

"Bro, you're so good," Ben told him.

"You think?"

"I know!" Ben confirmed.

Ben and RJ began walking out of the court together, away from the SUV and back to wherever RJ came from.

"Like, for real, bro. I could see you playing pro," Ben continued.

"Ah, you're lying. Stop gassing me, man."

"No gas. You're him," Ben said emphatically.

"Ayo, Ben!" Throne called out. "Where are you going?"

"I'ma head back with RJ. I'll catch up with you later." Ben turned without waiting for an okay.

"Works for me." Throne got in the SUV with Z and Frank drove them away. As they drove, Z looked out the window at Benjamin; he squinted and smiled.

"Whatcha smiling for?" Frank asked as he looked in the rearview mirror.

"Opportunity," Z responded.

"For what?" Throne asked.

"For that shrimp to make it out of here."

"I don't know about that tall basketball player, but as for Ben, homie, they did make it out," Throne commented.

"What do you mean?" Z asked, squinting intensely.

Throne adjusted himself in his seat and turned back to look at Z. "We found these boys spending their nights sleeping next to trash. They used cardboard to make a little hut for themselves; it's just up ahead, in the alleyway behind old Mr. Yu's restaurant."

"Can we check it out?"

"Their cardboard hut won't be there, but I guess we could show you the alley."

"Can we?" Z asked.

Throne raised his eyes to Frank. "Frank, can we make another stop?"

"Yeah, sure, Z. Whatever you need," he said as he drove the truck towards the alleyway behind the Chinese restaurant.

CHAPTER 17

"So, how'd you get so tall? Is your family tall? Grandpa tall? Great grandpa?" Ben asked RJ as he threw rocks at the ground. They walked to RJ's apartment complex where he lived with his mother.

"Nah, everyone in my family is kind of short," RJ said as he looked at the sky, still pondering the question. "Wait, my great grandpa might've been like six foot three or something."

"That's crazy. No way. You know, maybe you were adopted, dude."

"They have pictures with me right out of the womb. Don't talk like that. Now you sound stupid," he laughed at Ben.

"I ain't stupid," Ben said as he stopped walking.

RJ slowly stopped walking, rolled his eyes, and then turned to Ben, looking like he was exhausted from dealing with him. "I said you *sound* stupid, not you *are* stupid."

"Oh." Ben's narrowed brow relaxed as a smile returned to his face.

"But," RJ waited for Ben to continue walking. "You are stupid." RJ ran off immediately after saying it, laughing hysterically. Ben chased after him so angry it felt like his head would explode. But when RJ turned back, smiling from ear-to-ear, Ben's rage magically faded and he couldn't help but return the smile.

When they reached RJ's apartment complex, Ben was surprised by how nice it looked. It was a rather tall building with fancy stone architecture and even fancier people walking inside. The surrounding homes were residential and beautifully made. Hundreds of cars lined the streets and most of them were high end.

"Wow. Nice place."

"Yeah, I guess. Kinda used to it but it's because of my mom's job and all."

"What's her job?" Ben asked, genuinely curious.

"Honestly, I don't even know. Some government stuff."

"Makes sense."

"Yeah," RJ agreed.

"Well," There was an awkward silence for a second. "Well, I'll see ya, man." RJ initiated as he gave Ben a handshake.

"Yeah, for sure, man!"

Ben jolted after RJ had walked away. RJ turned and waved as he walked inside his apartment building. The glass door shut behind him and Ben watched until RJ disappeared from his view. Ben walked up closer and laid his face on the glass door, getting a better view inside the entrance hall. He saw expensive furniture and painted marbled floors, with crystal chandeliers that hung every ten feet or so at the ceiling of each corridor he could see.

I'm gonna live like this one day, Ben thought to himself. I'll make it. With Isaiah's help, I can make it for sure.

After checking out the alleyway where Benjamin and Isaiah used to live, Frank made a quick stop so Z could grab a few things and then they headed over to O-Time's place. Inside, O-Time sat on the couch as he was preparing to mail out packages of sealed marijuana and cocaine. The packages sat on the coffee table in front of him. He was finishing the last package as Throne opened the door.

O-Time's mother and aunt did not care that a gang used their house to run their business. It supplied money to pay the bills and protection.

Throne's role as big brother for O-Time gave them assurance that he would be okay, and it seemed like the business was growing with a promising future.

"So, where is this linebacker at?" Z asked as he sauntered inside behind Frank and Throne.

"Prolly upstairs," Throne answered as he flopped onto O-Time's couch.

"Who's that?" O-Time cranked his head back up. Immediately, his face lit up with a huge grin. "Hey! My long-lost brother!" O-Time yelled as he got up to greet Z. "What's it like to be a free man again?"

"Good O, good," Z laughed with him. O-Time patted his back and offered him a drink.

"Got a beer?"

"Of course, my brother." O-Time walked into the kitchen and opened the fridge. He reached in for a cold one, rattling the beer bottles together as he pulled one out.

"For the free man!" O-Time tossed the beer across the room to Z.

"Thank you."

O-Time nodded to Z.

A flush from the bathroom rang out and the door to it opened. Muscle P shuffled out and looked at Z, bewildered with his eyes popping out. "What in the! My man! Z! I knew it! I knew I knew that voice."

"How've ya been, P?"

"Same old same old, man. I can see you're doing well. I'm happy for you."

"Thank you, P."

The entire room was filled with joy and laughter as they welcomed their old friend back into the game. Arthur stopped by to say hello but had to work the night shift and left right after. Z was at O-Time's house catching up with the core group for about three hours. Not once did Isaiah come downstairs or show his face.

"Hey, Throne, are you sure that kid is here? How does he not come down to say hello?"

"Who? Isaiah? He was upstairs working on his breathing or some shit."

"Man does what?"

"Like for meditation I think."

"That boy meditates?"

"Must be why he's so level-headed," Muscle P added. Throne looked at Muscle P as if he had said something terribly wrong.

"Can someone get him for me?" Z asked the gang members in the room.

"Yeah, I got you."

O-Time jumped off the couch and headed upstairs. "Yo." O-Time knocked on the door. "Yo, Isaiah!" He knocked again and again and still, no response. "Hello?" Frustrated, O-Time opened the door to see Isaiah, who was about to open it himself.

"What is it?"

"Z, the guy who's been in jail, our homeboy, we've been hanging downstairs this whole time. He wants to talk with you and was asking for you specifically."

"Okay."

Isaiah followed O-Time down the stairs to see everyone in the living room. Z stood and looked at Isaiah. He was a bit surprised by his frame and size. Still, he asserted his dominance and stared into Isaiah's eyes with a cold stare. Isaiah returned the same look with more ferocity and spirit. For a split-second, Z looked down but immediately returned his gaze as Isaiah began to walk towards him. They shook hands, and

Isaiah took a seat on the couch. Muscle P slightly drifted to Isaiah's side as he sat down, submerging into the couch.

"You wanted to talk with me?"

"Yeah. What do you think of Benjamin?"

Isaiah sat up on the couch. "Ben is forever my brother."

"But it doesn't make sense. He's like a little chihuahua and you're built like a damn extra-large Pitbull. You got a 30-year-old prison body and this boy a straight twig, looking like a fourth grader. Shit don't make sense."

"Learn to not rely on your own understanding for the universe folds to no one but that which folds it."

The room was quiet.

"That shit don't make sense either."

The room erupted into laughter but returned to silence when Benjamin walked through the front door.

"Why is your man here tryna make shit philosophical for no reason?" Z called out to Ben.

Isaiah stood and said to Ben, "I was protecting your honor."

"My honor doesn't need protecting. What I need is something to smoke."

Mikey was sitting in the recliner and offered Ben a joint from behind his ear.

"Appreciate it."

"Got you," Mikey responded.

Isaiah scoffed and returned upstairs. He sat down in the room, closed his eyes, and began to breathe in and out slowly. He did so as he meditated on his God and planned a way to save Benjamin. As he did, the rest of them talked and laughed the night away, drinking and smoking until they all fell asleep where they were sitting.

Isaiah woke up extra early, quietly grabbed his pair of keys, made his way outside, and then jogged to the gym. Throne's gym was now where Isaiah and Ben slept when they were not at O-Time's place. Isaiah lifted weights for a few hours, took a shower, and prayed to his God as he started his day. It was always the same prayer.

"I ask for energy, will, and a strong mind. Please instill in me eternal love and praise. Protect Benjamin wherever he may go and watch over him always. Give me the strength to fight the demons he cannot. Amen."

CHAPTER 18

On a hot sunny Saturday afternoon, RJ and Ben were playing basketball together on the same court where they had first met. RJ was shirtless, revealing the one tattoo he had, which was prayer hands and a date under them. He and Ben had gotten closer over the past few weeks, and Ben discovered that it was for his baby sister, who died four years ago. Ben found it interesting how RJ was so human and real. He appreciated knowing that there were others dealing with something that wasn't always visible on the surface.

RJ instilled hope in Ben to push on and gave him the power and motivation he needed to overcome all that he faced. Ben had found confidence in his relationship with RJ. Ben saw himself as inferior to no one regardless of their standing, size, or ability.

"So, if you win, I give you one hundred dollars?" RJ asked, bouncing the basketball as he walked around the court.

"Yup," Ben answered.

"And if I win? Then what?"

"Bro, you're not gonna win. We have handicaps on so it will be a fair match."

RJ laughed, "Nah, I'ma win."

"Fine, what would you want if you happen to win?"

"Hmm. How about,,,"

"Yes?"

"I'm thinking, okay? Give me a second." There was a very long second before RJ said, "I got it!"

"What is it?"

"You gotta call me daddy for a week."

"What? No? I'm not doing that." Ben looked puzzled.

"Why? It's the truth."

"Shut up, loser."

"I'm not gonna win, you said it yourself. Why does it matter?"

Ben scratched his head, "Fine."

"There we go," RJ gave a menacing smile.

After a long and close game, Ben stood on the court defeated as RJ yelled, "That's game! I won!" He pumped his fist with joy.

"Damn," Ben said as sat on the floor. "This is gonna suck."

"Sure is." RJ laughed as he helped Ben off the floor.

"Oh, shut up."

"Shut up, who?" RJ laughed again. "You have to. It's a deal."

"Man, c'mon. That's too far."

"Not a man of your word, I see."

Ben groaned. "Fine." RJ laughed in anticipation. "Daddy."

RJ laughed even harder, "You actually said it! You called me daddy! Clown!" RJ shouted as he laughed some more. Ben was not amused, and soon, it became an ongoing joke with the gang.

Although RJ was not in the 21 Dragons, the core group recognized him. This new situation was an opportunity for RJ to tease Ben and he would bring it up every chance he got. As everyone enjoyed a laugh, Ben simply sat there and took it. Isaiah couldn't help but smile at the situation, but Ben was not amused.

CHAPTER 19

"I don't give a damn! Find them! Find them now!"

Connor stormed out of the control room, furious with his team's progress. The employees were left puzzled as they sat in front of their screens, monitoring Chicago city cameras. Connor was chief of this operation and the head of the agency. The operation manager was next in line and was waiting on orders from Connor in a remote safe house located somewhere in Illinois.

The operation was project D.O.N.U.T. It was a top-secret project created in the 1950s under the Eisenhower presidency. The place of operations started in New Mexico and had expanded over the years. Currently, six locations were spread across the world with the most active one hidden in the Sahara desert. That was where the majority of project D.O.N.U.T. took place.

From New Mexico to Tokyo, there had been underground structures created for mass transport. There were four massive tunnels with a height of a skyscraper and a width of a large lake, with each tunnel stretching thousands of miles long.

These four huge tunnels connected the six major bases located in New Mexico, America; the Sahara desert, Africa; Mount Yamantau, Russia; the North Sea, China; Tokyo, Japan; and London, UK.

Connor was furiously walking through the long white corridor of the base located in Africa. Hidden underneath the Sahara desert was a massive government facility funded by nearly every nation and underground market. Behind it all was Connor, the mastermind of C.I.M., a branch organization of the C.I.A., which expanded itself, growing in power and recognition. C.I.M.'s dominion of the American Government was a swift one since its formation sometime in the 1910s. Connor had guided C.I.M. to control not only the American government but all governments.

C.I.M., the Central Intelligence Maker, was responsible for mass government data, collection, and creation. It gave them the ability to tap into anyone's mobile phone or network and guide the general population to a problem or solution. It was technological warfare at its finest, herding not just the people of the U.S. but the people of the world. They weren't just technologically advanced with operatives working in every nation of the world to keep things under the supervision of C.I.M. This organization was trusted by leaders all around the world and the wealthy alike to keep them safe and in power.

"Connor!"

"What, Jason?" Connor barked back as he stopped pacing through the clean, futuristic looking hallway and turned to address Jason, his assistant.

"Connor, we need to talk about these applicants. These two boys from Chicago. We're using too many resources just to keep tabs on them. They aren't worth it; they're just a couple of rejects."

"What don't you understand when I say they are worthy applicants?"

"Look, I think they would make great candidates, too. From what we have studied, they have a high absorption rate, strong health levels, and absurd athletic intuition."

"So, what is there to talk about?"

"Aren't we rushing things? Plus, they have no technological connection. They essentially live off the modern grid."

"In what way are we rushing? And that's even better for us; no digital footprint to cover up afterward."

"Sir, we just finished the last round of applicants and none of them sufficed. We are wasting innocent lives, Sir," Jason spoke with a soft tone.

"We are wasting nothing but time. Sacrifices are necessary to achieve what we reach for here. Besides, we gather them for replacement. It is time, as the three have diminishing auras. We need three substitutes as soon as possible."

Conner turned away and Jason grabbed his hand. "Can we not wait for further maturation? They are so young."

Connor slapped Jason's hand away. "I could kill at six years old. A wolf is a wolf when it is born. A sheep is a sheep when it is born. My point is, you know how things are bound to be before they happen if you pay close attention. If you keep testing my decisions, you will no longer be involved."

"Yes, Sir. Sorry, Sir." Jason lowered his head and turned away.

Connor headed to his dark, secluded office, opened the globe, which sat on his desk, and pulled out a bottle of expensive bourbon. He grabbed a glass from under his desk and poured a shot. He began to sip the warm, comforting liquid as he leaned back and looked at the ceiling.

Connor let out a deep exhale and spoke into the air. "My mother would be ashamed of me."

"Yet your father is most definitely proud."

From out of thin air, a dark, cloudy deity appeared and sat down on the other side of Connor's desk. The dark clouds fell off the chair as a waterfall would a cliff.

"You knew my father? Why have you never told me?"

"You have never asked."

The deity seemed to be cloaked in a transparent darkness, which only revealed his figure and glowing yellow eyes.

CHAPTER 20

"Yo, Z."

"What's up?"

Both Z and Throne were on O-Time's couch rolling ground marijuana flowers mixed with crushed tobacco leaf into papers. They tucked and sealed them with their saliva and proceeded to burn them shut. They would then package them in plastic tubes as pre-rolled joints for sale.

"That kid, RJ, has been spending too much time around us," Throne said.

Z nodded. "I agree with you. Kid could be something special. Can't get stuck out here like us."

"We got to keep him away from the game. Could get him into trouble with some dangerous people. Damn, Ben the one dragging innocent bystanders into this."

"Ben needs respect. Not friends. He's got a brother in Isaiah. That's worth twenty friends."

"Damn straight."

They continued to talk about RJ and Benjamin as they finished rolling. Eventually, Throne shifted the focus back on the current plan and started talking about plans for the future: expansion throughout Chicago, creating something far bigger than the original purpose of 21 Dragons. The Throne pictured himself ruling Chicago and rivaling himself with legendary gangs like the Gangster Disciples and the Latin Kings.

"Just be careful, Throne. What you're implying means you're stepping on a lot of people's toes. Those gangs you envy to be like may stop you before you can even get there. It's a cruel, crazy world out here. Make sure you step with caution."

"I know, Z, I know. Appreciate you for looking out though. I'm gonna need you to make this work."

"For sure. I'm here to stay." Z smiled and dapped Throne up.

"Now, to get that RJ situation handled." Throne cupped his hands and used them to amplify his voice as he called upstairs. "Yo, Ben!"

"Yo!" Ben responded within seconds.

"Come down here real quick."

"Why?" Ben groaned at the top of the stairs.

Throne clicked his tongue and yelled louder, "Man, just get down here!"

"Fine." Ben reluctantly walked down the stairs, one by one as if his legs were filled with lead.

"Can't you just walk down the stairs already?"

"I am, my legs hurt," Ben groaned.

"Why?" Throne was reluctant to ask.

"Because I worked out today. It was leg day with Isaiah."

Z and Throne laughed. "Anyways," Throne began, "You gotta stop hanging out with RJ."

"What? Why?" Ben's tone went up immediately.

"Cause it's what he said," Z added.

Ben squinted at Z as if to say *this doesn't concern you*. "You ain't my father so don't tell me what to do," Ben snapped.

"You better watch yourself, shrimp." Z stood, towering over Ben, though Ben seemed unfazed.

"Besides, he's here right now."

"W-what?!" They both stammered in unison.

"RJ!" they yelled together.

"Wassup?" he responded.

"Get your ass down here, boy."

RJ walked down the stairs and entered the living room.

"Listen, man. We like you and you're a real one," Throne started, "but you can't stay around here. You've got potential; you've got a future. Stay as far away from this game as you can. Play the one you're good at. If you keep coming around here, you'll get linked up with us. It'll only make you a target—a six-foot nine target. Like, c'mon, man."

"If you don't want me around, be straight and just say that." RJ stormed out.

"Damn," Z palmed his face.

"That didn't go well." Z turned to Throne.

"Look what you did!" Ben yelled and then ran outside after RJ.

Throne chuckled to Z, "Yeah, that definitely didn't go as planned."

They began to laugh with each other. The two sat back down and resumed packaging pre-rolled joints.

The 21 Dragons were growing in popularity throughout Chicago. Everyone came to know The Throne, the self-proclaimed king of the Chicago streets, while other members of the gang were fairly known, like Z, Isaiah, Muscle P, Frank, and Arthur. The rest of the gang were not known and could not be identified by face alone. However, thanks to The Throne's tradition of initiations, the surrounding gangs and even simple citizens knew how to identify a member of 21 Dragons: the tattoo of a dragon on their right wrist or forearm.

Just as Ben caught up to RJ, a rival gang member of the 1500 gang noticed his flashy tattoo. The *1500* title had become saturated in its use throughout the streets and many gangs were not from the original 1500 gang. This particular 1500 gang was just that: a blend of wannabe thugs that were raised in a safe suburb community. With blue-collar ties and spoiled kids hooked on coke and Adderall, their largest consumers were college students.

This 1500 gang had been trying to sell on a street corner just a few blocks from RJ's apartment. However, it was difficult and risky. The member who spotted Ben wore a backwards red baseball cap. He was a white kid with a patchy beard, leaning against a pole smoking on a cigarette. The kid watched as Ben ran after RJ; he did not know either of them but they both stood out. The kid spit his cigarette out of his mouth and began to follow them with his hand on his waist ready to draw his gun.

"RJ, please, wait! Wait for me!"

RJ slowed down but continued to run. He turned to Ben and said, "No. They don't want me around. Not around them and not around you."

"Wait, wait just a second." Ben grabbed RJ's arm, but he swiped Ben's hand away. "This is so unlike you. Since when do you care what anyone thinks, anyways?"

"I don't care. But sometimes it just gets to me. I don't know, man. Forget it, seriously."

"Please."

"They don't need me. You don't need me. They're all assholes anyway. Why do you even hang with them? I'm just gonna go solo and focus on helping my mom."

"C'mon, bro, I need you. And it's complicated, man. I need them, too. I understand though. Family is important, or so I've been told."

"Man, fuck you. What are you talking about?"

RJ turned and began walking away from Ben. Ben chased after him again.

It was right before this point that the member of the 1500 gang caught up to them during their conversation. With a clear shot at Ben, who bore the gang affiliated tattoo, the kid aimed and fired. However, it was in this moment that RJ had turned and walked towards the gunman, unbeknownst he was walking right into the line of fire.

BANG.

Smoke poured out of the barrel of the 9mm pistol. As the shot echoed in the street, the 1500 gang member disappeared from the scene as quietly as he had arrived.

"RJ! RJ, no!" Ben cried, holding RJ up on his feet. RJ had been shot in the stomach and felt the blood leaking out of him. He touched the wound with his hand and lifted it up to his line of sight. A crimson red covered his fingers and he began to fall unconscious within moments. As he fell, Ben assisted his massive frame to the ground, gently.

"Help! I need help!"

Thankfully, Ben's screams for help drew a few bystanders who came rushing over to assist. After securing their help, Benjamin fled the scene, as well. He gave no information and believed he did his best to leave no trace of the 21 Dragons.

When Ben returned and updated the gang, it was determined that all communication needed to be cut off with RJ. They needed to leave him out of the game for good. Benjamin was reluctant, but knew it was for the best. They also decided it was necessary to hunt down whoever the shooter was, then show them how the 21 Dragons operated.

Against the gang's wishes, Benjamin and Isaiah secretly went to visit RJ in the hospital, making sure to hide their tattoos. They greeted RJ with care. Ben was sincerely sorry. RJ took the news of the gang's decision well, knowing it was for the best.

"I'll just see you at the park sometime, I guess."

"Yeah, bro, for sure." Ben smiled at RJ.

"Let's go," Isaiah said to Ben.

"Wait," RJ stopped them.

"Yes?" Ben asked.

"Isaiah keeps staring at the tattoo on my leg."

Isaiah walked up to him and openly examined the religious tattoo. "Yes, what does it stand for?"

"This is for my guardian angel. I pray to them for protection every night. Seems they were watching after Ben instead." RJ and Isaiah smiled.

"Wow," Ben said uneasily.

"Interesting. Why don't you pray to the creator directly?" Isaiah asked.

"My guardian angel carries my prayers for me. That's what I've grown up to believe."

"Interesting," Isaiah said with a thoughtful look.

"So, I assume that means you pray to God alone? Do you pray to Jesus or God or something else entirely?"

"Oh no, I don't pray to Jesus. I pray to the Creator alone."

"So, do you believe Jesus is God like my religion does?"

"Yes and no. The way my mind was created is complicated and the way I have interpreted the holy Bible is different from most people. If I tried to explain myself, it would take a month."

"You're a fascinating guy, Isaiah. Both of you are. I'm grateful to have met you."

Ben smiled and Isaiah nodded. They left RJ and the hospital quietly. Then, they stopped for a deli sandwich before returning to the gang at O-Time's house.

They arrived at the house a few hours later, only to discover that RJ had been murdered in his hospital bed by unidentified assailants. Simultaneously, both Ben and Isaiah knew that they must have been seen leaving RJ's room and it was assumed he was with 21 Dragons. The two boys were silent and shocked as they sat in the living room with the rest of the members who were called together for a mandatory meeting. None of them knew that they had visited RJ. And they weren't about to tell anyone. It slowly sank in while they sat there that it was their fault RJ was dead. They continued to keep their heads down and stare at the carpet. Suddenly, Throne's wild yelling brought them back to reality. He had gone berserk.

CHAPTER 21

"Who the fuck is responsible for this shit?" Throne yelled as he slammed his fist on the coffee table. Benjamin and Isaiah were stunned but kept their mouths shut. Throne was clearly under a lot of stress; his eyes were heavy and lifeless, yet hyper reactive and stone-cold. Arthur and Frank were behind him, silent as always. There was no telling what he'd do. The two boys had never seen him like this.

"Each and every one of y'all is a suspect. I need to know where your loyalty lies." Throne then looked at his gang as they all sat down in the living room. All of them were seated and attentive, except Z, who was still standing. Throne grabbed Z by the hand and broke one of his fingers with a quick snap.

"Shit!" Z grumbled as he pulled his hand away and cradled it in his other hand.

"The fuck was that, Throne?! You don't trust me?" Z remarked, his eyes turning into someone unrecognizable.

"I don't trust anyone." Throne took a step forward.

"So, what you're saying is you don't trust me." Z stepped forward as well and they got so close they could bump heads. "I respect you as the leader of this gang. My loyalty lies with The Throne. But if you ever touch me again, The Throne will be left empty."

Z held his ground, slightly taller than The Throne and significantly larger. Z pushed Throne and he lost his balance. Z stumbled for a second, and his eyes seemed eager for a fight. The room was tense, and no one else said a word, watching Z overpower The Throne by himself with a broken finger. Z's eyes faded back into their relaxed state. He walked away and sat down. Throne looked startled; he kept blinking as if he would wake from a dream. His mouth was open and his eyes wide, and in an instant, his ego returned. His mouth closed and his eyes lit up in a fury.

"Dumb bitch, what'd you say to me?" Throne pulled out a handgun and aimed it at Z.

"The fuck is the matter with you?" Muscle P yelled out as he, Akkun, Isaiah, and Benjamin jump for cover. Mikey crawled behind a chair while Frank and Arthur took a few steps back. Z stayed sitting as well, mean-mugging The Throne with a rich, arrogant look in his eyes. His body language was daring Throne to do something. His eyes were black and demon-possessed as he stared Throne down. In that moment, Z was ready to kill and Throne knew it.

Sweat was beginning to soak through Throne's shirt as he stood, looking down at Z. Every other second, he would wipe the sweat from his forehead with his free hand.

He aimed the gun at Z, with the barrel tilted to the side. His finger moved on and off the trigger, like a ticking time bomb waiting to explode. Throne took a step forward and extended his arm out in front of him, pointing it squarely. Z sat there, unfazed, seemingly prepared to take a bullet. He leaned forward with a sinister grin. "You better be prepared to kill me." Z's smile grew and his teeth showed; his eyes fixated on Throne's.

Throne stood there on the edge of killing one of his crew or losing all the respect he had garnered over the years. He swallowed hard as his finger moved back and forth onto the trigger. He slowly began to put pressure on it, seeing no other option until—

"Ayo! Put the damn gun down! This is my momma's house!" O-Time yelled, dropping his plate of jelly toast on the floor. "Damn. My toast." He bent down and picked it up to throw away. "Seriously though, y'all gotta do that outside or something. You know how my momma is."

"Yeah, tell 'em, O-Time! They're going crazy in here!" cried out Mikey in fear, still hiding behind the chair.

"Chill guys, chill." O-Time did not care about the fight or the guns; he simply didn't want it in the house. "C'mon, gang, you know we are not doing that here. My momma will beat my ass if she sees some bullet holes in the wall."

Z leaned back in his seat and slumped into a relaxed posture, eyes still alert. Throne put the handgun back in his pants and turned away from Z.

"We've been saying that we're riding with you and riding with 21 Dragons. What's with all this? You know that in God's name we'll fight for you," Muscle P said as they all took a seat.

"Yeah yeah. I gotta make sure of it. And Mikey, dude," Throne turned to little Mikey, "You cannot be crying like that if you're in this gang."

"I wasn't crying, yo."

"Nah, you definitely were," Ben chimed in.

"Chill, bro. He was pointing a gun at us."

"You still cried though."

The tense heaviness in the room lifted and Ben felt proud that he was able to restabilize the mood.

A few weeks passed since the incident, but it wasn't completely forgotten. Throne had cast doubt about Z's commitment, and he was even doubting himself. Z wanted it to be clear he was with them for good. Z was already a tree trunk of a man but the events that transpired ignited a desire to dominate those doubts. He decided he needed to get his chiseled prison body back. He began grinding for the next several weeks, changing his habits and schedule. With discipline, he steadily grew stronger, all to prove his loyalty to the group. When Z made a promise, he kept it.

Ben watched intently. Even though Z was submitting to The Throne, Ben knew who was the strongest and most influential in the gang. It wasn't just the obvious physical features. There was something about Z that made Ben want to change, as well. Ben began to see how fast Z put the muscle back on and shredded the fat off. Ben admired Z for his relentless pursuit and wanted to join the race himself. Z didn't mind coaching Ben with weights but training him was another story. Ben would ask daily to be mentored when Z was in the gym. Z would smile and say no, but would give Ben a tip to focus on. He didn't realize how serious Ben was. He wrote down every tip and memorized it, slowly putting it into action, either by himself or his time with Isaiah at the gym.

"Damn Ben, you're actually getting big," Z said to Ben one morning as Ben chased after him.

"Really?" Ben's eyes lit up. He had just gotten out of bed when he heard Z and had not put a shirt on yet. The extra fifteen pounds of muscle he had gained over the past two months showed. His young and developing body was looking toned and strong.

"Yeah, really," Z smiled as he responded. "Keep it up and I might just train you."

Ben's smile reached from ear to ear and he walked with Z to his car. Z got in his car and started the engine. Ben was still smiling and staring at Z through the driver's window. Z, almost annoyed, lowered the window. "What? Why are you smiling?"

"Oh sorry." Ben wiped the grin off his face the best he could.

"What are you waiting for?" Ben was starting to get on Z's nerves.

"I'm waiting for my tip," he said innocently.

Z smiled, "Nah. No tip today." He laughed, "In fact, you know, that's enough for now. The only thing I can tell you now is to never take your foot off the gas."

With that, Z smashed on the gas pedal and sped off, leaving Benjamin coughing in a dust cloud. Benjamin ran into the building to wake Isaiah, who was up and meditating, seemingly waiting for Benjamin to come get him.

"To the gym?" Isaiah asked.

"You read my mind." Ben smiled as they walked together into the gym from their sleeping quarters.

It was late in the day and they had finished all of their drug runs. The three of them, Akkun, Benjamin, and Isaiah, sat on a curb and smoked a joint. Isaiah did not smoke but he tagged along. "Bro, I'm telling you." Akkun took a long pull off his joint. He looked up to the sky and blew the smoke out of his lungs and into the night sky. "These big corporations essentially keep the world running. There are some higher ups, like a bunch of greedy assholes who run this world for their benefit. They have different nations on their side that may even hate each other but each nation submits to them. They control these government agencies and have a deep interest in the United States. The environmental agencies who are supposed to protect the people are corrupt and even give in to these people in fear or out of worship."

Benjamin just started laughing. Isaiah was quiet and still.

"Bro I'm serious about this shit. I've done mad research."

Benjamin snatched the joint from Akkun's hand. "Yeah, you don't need that anymore." Benjamin started laughing and stood.

Isaiah randomly spoke up, "Instead of stressing over the government and the nations, why not stress over your existence? Think of it like this—"

Benjamin interrupted Isaiah, "Oh, c'mon, not another lesson, brother."

"Just wait. Hear me out. Think of the universe like a thought bubble. You are a being, by yourself, and then you have a thought. That thought bubble is a universe inside your mind that you created. I think that is what the universe is—what *we* are. We are simply the imagined universe of God. At any given moment, all of reality can cease to exist because the thought is ended."

"Man, you're crazy," Akkun snickered.

"Like, for real. You don't even know the half of it. Zero drugs involved in his thinking," Ben added as they stood on the curb watching the dancing street lights.

CHAPTER 22

The next week, Z was found dead. Akkun quit the gang in front of The Throne. He didn't care about the consequences. He was more terrified of dying in the streets than he was afraid of what the self-proclaimed king might do to him. He was right. Throne let him walk free with no consequences, except being banished from the gang. The rumor was that Z got killed in a gang-related shooting. According to O-Time's source, he was ambushed, and they were all wearing masks. Apparently, they were part of the 1500 gang. Supposedly, Z was approached and confronted for sleeping with seven women who had been sexed-in with the gang. Z had been using the loft upstairs and knew the owner. It was mostly for storage but on occasion, the owner would allow Z to sleep there. Z had taken all seven women up with him that night.

It wasn't until one by one, the women came downstairs that the gang members took notice. By the time all the gang members were looking, Z was following close behind the last lady, guiding her off the steps with his hands on her voluptuous ass. They did nothing at the local bar but yell at their women and call them slurs. Then, later, they followed Z when he left. Z went into a fast food restaurant and sat down to enjoy a burger. Seven members of the 1500 gang rushed in wearing black ski masks, dressed completely in black. Each put a bullet in his chest and then quickly fled the scene, leaving no trace. But someone was arrogant enough to brag about the details, leaking the information. No one expected the cops to respond but the 21 Dragons had already began to develop a plan to exact their revenge.

Benjamin sobbed alone in the gym bathroom, assuming no one was in the building. But Throne was there, adding money to the safe he kept in the gym office. Throne entered the bathroom.

"Nah, shrimp, don't act like that. What? Are you some type of bitch?"

"What? When did you get here?" Ben asked quietly.

"I've been here. Why are you crying, man?"

"I was becoming good friends with Z. I looked up to him, man. He had status. I wanted to get stronger with him."

"You're saying that you need friends to get stronger? You couldn't be further from the truth."

"Don't you need friends to have your back and support you?" Ben pleaded.

"Yeah, man, yeah. You need a couple friends in general, just in case, ya know. But to win, to make it big, all you need is yourself and your strap. Listen, shrimp, ain't nobody fucking with me because I'm a veteran at this shit. Listen to me and you'll get where you wanna go, enough to leave this concrete jungle. Your friendships will only hold you back. All you need is you, not me, not Z, and not Isaiah, either."

Ben stiffened up at the thought of not having Isaiah to help him.

"In fact, real gangsters stand alone. Are you a gangster or not?"

"I'm a gangster," Ben squeaked.

"Oh, sure, shrimp." Throne laughed at Ben.

"Sure," Ben mumbled.

Throne smiled, flashing the three gold teeth in his mouth. He turned around to walk out but continued, "If you wanna be like me, you gotta live like a savage. You gotta let yourself drown in pain to find out if you can breathe underwater. I damn sure can!"

Then, he walked out, leaving Ben alone. Ben waited in the bathroom for a few minutes, listening for Throne to leave the gym. He stared at the leaking faucet as each droplet splashed into the sink while a disturbing thought grew. It was the chilling sense of losing Isaiah to grow stronger.

Flashing jewelry and money, The Throne always had attention, status, and girls. He was respected and feared, not by all but by enough. That was the type of power Ben wanted. He didn't want to be dead inside like Throne, but he envied the way he commanded respect with his presence. Ben wanted everyone to be afraid of his power, to make a path when he walked, and most of all, to see the red carpet rolled out for him. He wanted to taste all that the world had to offer, but he wanted the easy way there. No suffering. Ben stayed in the gym, thinking over what Throne had said. He decided to rest on the gym office couch.

Not knowing how long he was there, he heard Isaiah come in. He greeted Benjamin with a smile and asked, "What's up?" Ben just shook his head, then Isaiah grew serious. "First RJ and now Z. This is getting out of control," Isaiah said as he looked at Ben, who was still lying on the couch. "Ben?" Ben was unresponsive, staring at the wall with lifeless eyes. "You okay?" Isaiah leaned in and tried to comfort him, placing his arm over Ben's shoulders. The life in Benjamin's eyes instantly resurfaced when Isaiah's hand touched his shoulder. It was as if a fog had cleared and the cloudy film was lifted from the his eyes.

"Sorry, what'd ya say?"

"No need for an apology. I just wanted to make sure you're alright."

"Oh, yeah. Yeah, I'm good. I just, I—" There was a moment of silence as Ben gathered his thoughts. "I literally talked with Z like last week. He said he was going to start training me. Now, he's gone. Just like that."

Isaiah said nothing. He sat in silence with Benjamin.

"Like, it's unfair, man. It's unfair. Where's this god of yours? Isn't he supposed to help us out?" Isaiah stayed quiet and allowed Benjamin to dump everything out of his system. "God's fake. He isn't real. Bad things wouldn't happen if he was. Z would still be here. Fuck god. Fuck that 1500 gang! I'll kill 'em all."

Finally, Isaiah spoke. "I understand how you feel. Our life is but a vapor in this world. Life on earth is truly unfair. However, if bad things weren't supposed to happen, then that means we aren't supposed to be here. My God has a plan to use all these bad things that happen for some greater purpose. Taking a life for a life just leaves us with more loss. Think about what you say." Isaiah challenged him and then waited for his response.

"I am thinking. I'm thinking of avenging Z. There is no greater purpose; there is only death after life." With that, Benjamin stormed through the front door, leaving Isaiah feeling hopeless as he sat on a stool with his hand on his head.

The Throne had asked the members to meet at the gym. Sixteen men and eleven kids gathered, all wearing black ski masks and black clothing. Most of them carried handguns, though some had shotguns or semi-automatic submachine guns. The Throne quieted the room and then announced war with the 1500 gang, who were responsible for killing Z.

"The 1500 gang, which attacked Z, are now also suspected to be responsible for the killing of RJ. We will get these stupid assholes. I got word that their gang is together at one of their homes near Rockford. We'll take five of our vans and load everyone up. Once we get there, it'll have to be quick. Tonight, we will show them who is in charge. Everyone in these streets will know why you don't mess with the 21 Dragons."

They all shouted in agreement, flashing their guns and fists in the air. Some pulled up their sleeves and pointed to the dragon tattoo on their right wrist. The room had an intense weight to it, which was fueled by the mad bloodlust that permeated from them. The core members, along with Mikey, Benjamin, and Isaiah, were there together with all the new members.

"Whatcha doing, Isaiah?" Benjamin asked. He had walked away from the crowd and over to Isaiah, who sat on a bench in front of a massive mirror, which extended through most of the gym.

"I only do these things for you." Isaiah stood and brushed the dust off his pants. "Is it time to go?" Isaiah asked.

"Yeah." Ben was in shock. He never expected Isaiah to tag along, not for this.

The usually lively streets were quiet and empty. No one but the 21 Dragons gang knew what was about to unfold. A strange darkness consumed the night and plagued the air with evil thoughts. Five cars with the license plates removed pulled up in unison to the home in Rockford. The area was quiet yet music and lingering smoke came from the front window of the house. Before the cars could come to a complete stop, all the passenger doors swung open. Gang members scattered and surrounded the house within moments. Isaiah waited in the car with Mikey as instructed by Frank and Arthur. Throne told Ben to wait as well but he rushed in beside him and Throne allowed it to happen.

Six members of the small 1500 gang were in the house. After Throne and Arthur signaled to each other, they moved into the house from the front and back doors. Isaiah and Mikey heard gunshots go off. Then, a barrage of shots followed until it calmed down and one last shot was heard. Seconds later, the members of 21 Dragons were in their cars, driving away.

Isaiah counted nine shots in total. It was a perfectly devised plan and they executed six members. They didn't even have a chance to arm themselves.

A few minutes later, seven police cars with an ambulance arrived at the scene, sirens blaring. The responding officers routinely investigated the scene to find five dead kids. One had survived—the only female of the group, who was shot in the neck. Weapons, drugs, and even more damning evidence was found at the scene. The police determined it was gang-related. There were no witnesses and the security camera footage they found didn't help. The cops arrested the surviving member. Once she was fully recovered, she gave up the names of the other members and connections to plead her sentence down. Without further evidence, they could not link the shooting to any group or gang. However, the 21 Dragons had taken ownership and it was creating a stir on the streets. Detectives began to keep tabs on the gang the best they could. Throne had expected this and trained his members to move with more caution and secrecy. With his reputation growing, Throne was now known throughout Chicago by gangs and law enforcement alike.

While Throne's name was becoming infamous, other members' names were surfacing as well, like Muscle P, Frank, and Isaiah. Benjamin's name was stagnant, even with all the effort he put in; no one showed him the respect he so badly wanted.

Ben grew envious of Throne over the next few years. Obvious to everyone including Throne was his drive for power and money. Over time, he grew strong and tall, training harder than ever before. He was training to be like Z, emulating Z's life to become one of the strongest members of the gang. Ben was no longer a runner but a distributor. He'd already learned enough about the streets and had established loyal customers. He focused on knowing his competitors and figuring out how to beat them. Eventually, Ben established some respect, but not the level of respect he desired. Benjamin and Isaiah were now sixteen years old.

The core of the gang hadn't changed much, though the gang had significantly grown in number. Their profit and status positioned them as one of the major gangs in Chicago. Still, Throne kept seeking expansion; nothing was ever enough for him.

Muscle P now went by his birth name, Pedro. He had become lazy and stopped training. Isaiah was now well known for his extraordinary feats of athleticism and bravery. He won every fight, regardless of how many people he fought. It seemed that when he showcased his God-given talent of strength, people were awestruck. The streets even compared him to the legendary myth of a man, John Henry, the American folk hero who beat the steam drill, which was said to be an impossible feat. When asked about his strength, Isaiah always admitted it was simply genetics. Often, he wondered why he was gifted with such a large and powerful frame. Isaiah always arrived at the same conclusion: he was here for Benjamin.

That year, gang violence reached a historically high point across the entire country, especially in Chicago. The United States was now governed by a dictatorship; there were constant school shootings, political unrest, horrific natural disasters that had taken their toll on the economy, and tension between supporting nations. The world seemed to be eroding at its societal core, and each nation grew increasingly divided. World laws for tackling climate change were overturned in some nations and completely ignored in others. With increasing global emissions and no plans in place to reduce the use of fossil fuels, air pollution had now killed millions. In Chicago, without police presence, the streets were unsafe. City safe havens became the places to live in the United States, though they were controlled by the dictatorship and very selective.

Benjamin and Isaiah rekindled their promise to be there for each other, keenly aware of their mutual loss of RJ and Z. They had reached a pinnacle in their street life and it left them feeling empty. They decided they wanted out. Somehow, they would find a way out of this city and find a way to do anything but this.

Tyrone was now known as The Throne to everyone in Chicago. The silent Latin Kings had finally had enough of his enormous ego. The Latin Kings snatched up Akkun and he was forced to reveal everything he knew about the 21 Dragons. He became their mole and informant while the Latin Kings waited for the right time to strike. They sent scouts from the gang to confirm Akkun's reports. As the Latin Kings stalked the 21 Dragons, there were others lurking even more secretive in the shadows, closely watching.

Benjamin and Isaiah had finally been identified and located. The two boys fit the program perfectly. For the past several years, CIM dispatched CIA agents across the state of Illinois in search of them. A year ago, agents patrolling the Chicago area had found Benjamin and Isaiah. For the past several weeks, the agents noticed other stalkers, particularly the Latin Kings. following them, as well. They did nothing but watch, tracking the two boys, observing the crime and violence. The agents continued to focus their job on just surveillance. As commanding chief, Connor was busy orchestrating a massive mosaic of madness that would impact the human race in its entirety.

The Latin Kings were ready and prepared, growing excited about the fact that the self-proclaimed king of the streets, The Throne, would be struck down.

"Let's just kill these scumbags already," Zipper said as the massive gang spread across an entire city block.

"Establecer a mi amigo cremallera[5]," El Diablo, leader of the Latin Kings, responded.

"I'm sorry, Diablo. I'm just so sick of waiting."

"I understand your urge, my friend. Patience."

"But what are we waiting on?"

"Throne is on the move with Frank, Pedro, and O-Time. We must wait until they have returned. Then, while they are all assembled together, we take them out in one swoop. Arrancarles la puta cabeza!⁶" El Diablo screamed into the sky and all the men began to do the same. The block sounded like a jungle, in which every animal was filled with immense anger and power. The spirit of the group came together as one powerful entity, ruling over their souls, preparing them for this moment, and commanding a wild rage that would fuel their execution of the 21 Dragons.

Throne, Frank, Pedro, and O-Time were in Hammond, Illinois, visiting a well-respected group who had thrived in this desolate economy and overpowering dictatorship. Even though The Throne now owned many businesses and monopolized the drug running throughout the city, he still wanted more. On a decent week, this group of professionals would pull in about twenty times the profit Throne could make in a month. The group had ties to some of the richest diplomats in the world. Throne was at an all-time high; he was in his prime but he would often say he was just getting started. With his confidence and most trusted members by his side, he believed that a deal with these professionals was attainable.

During this trip away, the gang let their guard down. They had become lazy, and no longer reflected the reputation that had built the 21 Dragons. Gone was the tight-knit group with matching tattoos. They resembled more of a large group of criminals, who simply wanted to have fun and notoriety while they terrorized the city of Chicago. The

---

⁵ "Calm down Zipper, my friend."
⁶ "Rip their fucking heads off!"

members didn't push sales and when they did, it was done improperly. While The Throne was away focusing on building the business, things got even worse. With only Arthur left in charge, the members rebelled. Focused on getting out, Ben and Isaiah had removed themselves from the day-to-day involvement of the gang. The core of the 21 Dragons had deteriorated and the leadership of the gang was fragile. Rumors about Ben and Isaiah's plans were circulating. The gang's inward aggression surfaced as hostility among the ranks grew.

CHAPTER 23

"El Diablo, may I speak with you?"

At a rather luxurious home, El Diablo sat with two women on his lap. Zipper was asking for a one-on-one discussion with the leader of the group, the Latin Kings. El Diablo groaned as he motioned the two beautiful Mexican women away, and stared at their naked sauntering hips as they left the room. Slowly, he turned to Zipper, a stern expression replacing his lust.

"Que es, mi amigo?[7]"

"We need to attack now. Their drug runners act as if our name does not hold tremendous weight. Make them mad so they hurry back. Then kill them while they make a foolish mistake. Asustemos a estos novatos.[8]"

"Vamos a matar pronto a mi amigo.[9]"

"¡Ahora![10]"

El Diablo stood from his plush couch and leaned into Zipper, snarling into his ear.

"Don't get loud with me. We go when I say."

---

[7] "What is it my friend?"

[8] "Let's scare these newbies."

[9] "We are going to kill them soon my friend."

[10] "Now!"

"Sì senor," Zipper answered and began to walk off.

"So, go! Show them whose territory this truly is." El Diablo grinned and Zipper did, too, finally able to relieve himself of at least some of his built up bloodlust.

"El trono será nuestro.[11]"

Zipper sent word to find one of the drug runners of the 21 Dragons and bring them to El Diablo.

They were not done with Akkun. Now under the command of the Latin Kings, he was known to the gang as a traitor and a snitch; they controlled his every move. Even though Akkun betrayed the 21 Dragons and followed the orders of El Diablo, no one from 21 Dragons was aware. Still welcomed by the group and considered trustworthy, his best friend was Mikey. Mikey was a drug runner who knew the city like the back of his hand, and whose fast legs could outrun anyone. His kind heart wasn't meant for this harsh lifestyle. However, he found joy running drugs and being out on the street all day. He was content with his role and didn't feel a need to progress to anything else. He often said he could be a runner for life as long as he was with the gang.

"Mikey." Mikey turned around, looking in all directions for the familiar voice. "Psst. Mikey. Psst," Akkun called out from an alley.

Mikey backed up slightly and looked into the alley. With an astonished look on his face, he responded. "Akkun? Akkun is that you?"

"Yeah, it's me, Mikey. It's Akkun."

"Where have you been?" Mikey said with a smile.

"Trying to stay out of trouble," Akkun responded.

"Is that why we haven't seen you around?" Mikey asked.

"Yeah. Now, I need your help."

---

[11] "The Throne will be ours."

"My help? Why?"

"You're the only guy I can trust."

"What is it?" Mikey reluctantly asked.

"I need you to follow me," Akkun said with his head down, unable to look Mikey in the eyes.

"Bro, I'm in the middle of a carry right now. Can this wait?" He chuckled at the obvious.

"It's like that? We haven't seen each other in how long?"

"Bro, c'mon. You know how it is. I'll catch up with you later, where ya gonna be?"

Akkun scoffed, "Still Throne's mule I see."

"Man," Mikey clicked his tongue. "You ain't know shit about it. You left us for a while? Your ass is still over here begging for help. Shit ain't changed for you either."

"Fuck you!"

"You ain't even worth it." Mikey turned away to continue his route.

"You're right about that." Two massive Mexican men with tattoos covering their bodies stood in Mikey's way. "This kid isn't worth anything. He set you up for a trap. What a friend."

Akkun turned away, unable to watch what he knew was coming next. The two massive men knocked Mikey unconscious and tossed his body into a black van as if he were a bag of garbage. Another appeared and stood behind Akkun with his hand on his shoulder. Akkun felt a tingling sensation rise in his spine as the man spoke.

"You know we can't have you around anymore doing something like that, right?" Akkun began to cry but pistol whipped unconscious before a tear could emerge.

The next day, Mikey's body was found hanging from a bridge. Akkun's lifeless body swung beside Mikey's, both restrained from the neck. The Latin Kings had spray-painted their name on the bridge from where they hung, claiming the murder and declaring war on the 21 Dragons.

CHAPTER 24

"Sir," Jason said into the burner phone blocks away from the CIA van.

"Yes, Jason," a deep and annoyed voice answered. "This better be good."

"Yes, Sir. Of course, Sir. That's why you sent me here. To ensure an extraction of the target." Jason waited a moment to see if Connor would say anything. Then, he continued. "We have eyes on the two targets, the specimens you wanted. They have distanced themselves from the gang, which was our previous problem. Once they are active again, we will observe until the right moment to initiate extraction."

"That is good news, Jason. Proceed with the mission."

"Yes, Sir."

The call ended and Jason removed the battery from the phone, broke the phone in half, and tossed them in two separate trash bins as he walked back towards the CIA surveillance van. Inside the van, behind the driver and front passenger seat, hid four tech operatives running social media, audio, and video surveillance for the neighborhood, all aimed at capturing Isaiah and Benjamin, the two homeless runaway orphans.

"Why do we put so much effort for a couple of kids?" The man sighed and stared at the ceiling of the van, bored with his job.

"No one told you?" A female operative spun her chair around to face him.

"Don't you know?" Another operative turned to him.

"I clearly don't know, so can you just fill me in?"

The woman who turned to him first began to explain. As she did, she was moving her hands around to get her point across. "While we are CIA operatives, we actually work for CIM, which is essentially the behind-the-scenes dictator for 90% of the countries across the world. This massive undercover operation, which runs the world, is headed by the man who Jason just went to take a call with. Therefore, this operation is highly sensitive and highly confidential."

"Okay, I know all that."

"Alright, so what you don't know then is that this operation is for Project D.O.N.U.T.S., also referred to as the S.S.T.F."

"I've heard rumors of Project D.O.N.U.T.S., but what is the S.S.T.F.?"

"The super soldier training facility," the other operative stepped in.

"What? Where?"

"Top secret. No one knows," the woman said.

"Wait, so we're making super soldiers for the U.S. now?"

"Scientists have been doing that for some time now; however, C.I.M. claims to have perfected it, though no one said it was for the U.S."

"I never knew this shit. And what's this Project Donut? Same thing? What's with the name?"

"It's the name of the project that governs the facility where they create these super soldiers. I don't know why it's called donut." She laughed and put her headset back on, spinning her chair back to face her monitor.

The black CIA van went undetected for the remainder of their surveillance. Once Jason returned, they began to instruct the two field agents to the targets.

"Both targets have been spotted; check your maps. They have been updated."

"Copy that." An agent on the streets lowered his watch away from his mouth and ended the call. With a tap on the watch, he went into maps mode, which had two red moving dots on the screen, representing the boys' location. The agent then called the other field agent and they met up a few blocks closer to the targets. They wore sunglasses, beanies, jeans, leather jackets, and boots. They did not walk next to each other yet took similar routes to the targets.

Isaiah and Benjamin were laughing with each other when they noticed the two field agents, even though they were separately approaching them from different sides of the street. Immediately, they turned into an alley and started running. When the agents made it to the alley, they saw Isaiah and Benjamin just as they split up. The two agents were forced to split up as well. Ben ran across the street and into another alley. Isaiah just turned the corner and ran straight; the agent could not catch up with him. Ben ran out of the second alley and turned right towards Isaiah. The agent was catching up to Ben but lost the visual as Ben turned the corner. Twenty feet ahead of Ben was a very young boy riding a bike. Ben accelerated to his top speed and pushed the kid off the bike and onto the pavement. Before the child could say anything, Benjamin was gone, pedaling harder than ever before. Even though Ben could not hear him, he still screamed and began to throw a temper tantrum. As he stomped on the sidewalk, the CIA agent ran past him at full speed, trying to catch up to Benjamin. It was futile and Ben turned back at him, sticking his tongue out.

The agents regrouped and reported back to the van. "We lost them; we are in pursuit again."

All the members in the van groaned.

Jason yelled to the agents, "Find them. They cannot be far." Jason ended the call. The driver began to move the van closer to their moving targets. This time, Jason devised a plan to trap them in an alleyway.

Where is he? Isaiah thought to himself as he waited in their old alley hideout behind Mr. Yu's restaurant.

"Right here," Ben announced as he walked into the alley, somehow reading Isaiah's mind. "Miss me?" Ben said with a smug face.

"Sure," Isaiah laughed. "If that makes you feel better."

"How long were you waiting for me?"

"I don't know, like five minutes. Not long."

"Cool. So, who do you think those guys were?"

"I honestly have no idea. I could only assume the Latin Kings, the ones who killed Akkun and Mikey. Though they would have just killed us, right?"

"We gotta get outta these streets, Zay."

"I know. I've been saying this. It's getting too crazy now."

"So, how? If they know what we look like, they will just find us again and again."

"Let me think." Isaiah rubbed his chin.

"Okay, genius, think."

Isaiah gave him a side eye, rolled his shoulders, and turned away. After a minute, he looked at Benjamin. "Okay," Isaiah began. "I think we take all the money we have saved and—"

"I already spent it." Ben's head hung low.

"How? On what?" Isaiah clicked his tongue.

"Dumb shit."

"Like what?"

"Like bets, food, drugs."

"I knew it. You're an addict, bro."

"I kinda am. That's why we gotta get outta here."

"Alright, so new plan."

"Great."

"New plan is that we go to the police and tell them everything. Get witness protection and a home."

"Then, what about the gang? You wanna be a snitch?"

"No, but what other options do we have?" Ben's eyes drew a blank and he stared into the distance. "Can you hear me? Ben?" Isaiah waved his hand in front of Ben's face. "You okay?"

Ben snapped back to reality. "Sorry." He shook his head.

"Don't say sorry. We'll get out somehow. We don't have to go to the police."

They sat down in silence and threw pebbles at the alley wall as they thought about a way out of Chicago.

"The Throne. He's gone," Ben's eyes lit up.

"So?"

"So, no one is guarding the safe where he keeps the new office."

"Ben." Isaiah's spine shivered, "Please, stop. Someone else is guarding it."

"Yeah, some bums we don't even know who shouldn't even be in the 21 Dragons."

"Ben, it's not funny."

"I'm not laughing; it's our only chance of getting out." They silently stared at each other. Ben continued. "I know where the safe is. It's in the new building he bought, the one that sells auto parts or something. I know the blind spots for the security cameras. I know how to get in."

"I don't know, man."

"Think about it. Besides that, do you wanna camp out here tonight?"

"Not a bad idea. The Latin kings have no idea that we started right here. Nowhere is safer," Isaiah responded.

"Tomorrow will be our last day here in Chicago, no matter what."

"Agreed," Isaiah said. They shook on it and prepared for themselves a bed of cardboard. The boys laid down beside each other and began to drift off. Even though it was midday, they fell fast asleep and rested like babies. Isaiah smiled in his sleep as he could not contain the joy he felt being away from the gang but still with his brother.

Meanwhile, in Connor's dark office, he sat yet again at the end of another long day, sipping on his bourbon and thinking about what the yellow-eyed devil had said.

"Why do you keep bothering me when I try to drink?" Connor had felt a sudden shift in the air.

"You know you won't get drunk."

"I can still try."

The deity laughed in the shadows.

"Why laugh?" Connor asked.

"You act just like these mortals."

"I am half mortal."

"You can be so much more."

"Like my father?"

"Your father was arrogant. He had everything, still, he willingly broke his contract."

"To create me."

"To show your mother temporary love before abandoning her, leaving to the depths of hell forever, where he is restrained by chains in a furnace so hot it melts his soul while simultaneously restoring it, keeping him in a constant state of torture."

Connor poured himself another double. "I don't really need to get into those details."

"My apologies; it gives me pleasure to imagine such a thing."

"I can see that," Connor laughed. "Still, I want this power you speak of."

"I know you do. I've seen the preparations you've made for the ritual. You will attain unimaginable strength, speed, endurance, knowledge, and instinct. So much power that you could rival even an arc angel."

Connor salivated at the opportunity to truly rule this world—not just behind the scenes as some mastermind villain, but as a majestic and unstoppable god supported by the CIM and ultimately, the world.

CHAPTER 25

The rain beat sideways from the dark clouds covering the Chicago streets. The wind tore at the cardboard as they huddled under the flimsy protection that spread across two dumpsters. Dirty and shivering, the boys contemplated their plight. Having awoken to the rain after their long nap, the torrents of water were now spilling off the sides of the soaked cardboard. Then, a strong wind from the storm blew the cardboard roof away, revealing the hopelessness reflected in their eyes. Isaiah had been debating whether they should try to steal from The Throne. The plan was becoming far less complicated and difficult. His hunger for an escape from this life had permeated his thinking.

"Look, Isaiah, it's easy; quick in and out. I know you're thinking about it."

Ben turned to Isaiah with water running down his face. Isaiah turned away and exclaimed, "Ben, are you crazy? Do you really wanna die! Is that what you want? Look how dangerous this place is, man. Akkun and Mikey, they were just kids like us," Isaiah replied.

"No, obviously not, Zay, but Throne still isn't here; he's outta town and his stash is guarded by those lowlifes. C'mon, Zay, this is our chance. We can finally get out of here with that money," Ben begged.

Isaiah paused and pondered all the money in his head, imagining all they could accomplish if they were rich. There would be a future for his brother rather than being stuck in the trenches. Even with the risk, this seemed to be the best option to get out fast.

Isaiah turned to the wall of the alley and thought. He was wearing a dark blue hoodie paired with black sweatpants. His sneakers were completely worn down to reveal the last layer of red. He thought about what he had and what he was missing. What he wanted and what he was stuck with. Most of all, he thought about how he could change all that. Isaiah decided at that moment that he was going to do the unthinkable. His decision showed in his facial expression. Excitement built up inside him, his teeth showing from his smile. He was now consumed with the idea. With a fierce swing of his torso, he faced Ben, clenched his fist, and held it out. Ben smiled at Isaiah and said, "I knew you'd come along."

"Only because I don't want you to die alone."

The two bumped fists and grinned with determination.

They planned their mission, carefully going over the treacherous details. Throne had his safe house on East 132 street. Benjamin and Isaiah discussed going through the ventilation to enter the abandoned factory. Then, each carrying a bag, they would choose different paths to confuse the men and meet up at the bus station afterward.

Benjamin and Isaiah squeezed their way through the tight silver vents into a room on the second floor. The room was empty and unfinished, with hardwood flooring on the right side patiently waiting to be nailed to the ground. They quietly opened the stained wooden door and peeked their heads out into the hallway. With no one in sight, they looked at each other and nodded as reassurance to move ahead. They started tiptoeing down the hallway to the one door that was cracked open. As they looked in, they saw the safe. The door was mistakenly left unlocked, leaving the safe unprotected. Walking into the room, they glanced back into the hallway to make sure they weren't being watched. Ben shut the door behind himself, quietly and softly.

Isaiah slowly reached into the vault and pulled out a large airtight bag filled with a white substance.

"Oh shit…that's crack!" said Ben in shock.

"Yes," Isaiah assured him, holding a large bag of a whitish mineral-like substance.

"Wow! Look at all that money," Ben remarked.

"It's a lot, for sure." Isaiah tossed the bag aside.

At that moment, Ben covered Isaiah's mouth and softly spoke into his ear. "Shhh, listen."

Isaiah was clearly annoyed but listened to the sound of footsteps coming up the stairs, echoing through the hallway and into the eardrum of Isaiah's keen hearing.

"Check who it is," whispered Isaiah.

Ben looked through a small crack in the door to see a tall and skinny light-skinned man with an assault rifle coming up the stairs. The man began to walk their way.

"Someone with a gun is coming here," Ben spoke softly.

"Let's go," Isaiah whispered as he began to pack the money into a bag.

Dragging his feet up the stairs, the man was annoyed. They had been playing poker and he was sitting out so he was sent to check on a noise they had heard.

"Why me?" he said with a deep voice.

"'Cause you're not playing; remember, I'm in charge now that Tyrone is gone," said the tattooed white guy with black sunglasses too big for his head.

"Ugh, fine."

As he made his way down the hallway, he saw an open door on the far side and headed toward it. He slowly opened the door to see the safe wide open along with the window and rain pouring inside. He rushed to the window to see the two boys midair as they jumped for it into the dark night. They landed and then rolled gracefully onto the pavement, despite how slippery it was from the water.

When they landed, the man saw Isaiah's bag overflowing with cash and yelled as the boys took off running. "Get the two boys outside; they stole Throne's money!"

Immediately, the men jumped up, chairs crashing backward, knocking over the poker table and sending cards and chips flying. Grabbing their handguns, they took off outside in pursuit to see the boys not far ahead of them.

"They're behind us, four of them," Ben said to Isaiah.

"Okay, let's split up now."

"Are you sure?"

"Yes, now! Quick, go!" Isaiah commanded Ben.

They ran in separate directions, hoping to escape their sight.

"Which one do we go for?" said one of the men as they paused to ponder the decision before stopping and picking a direction.

"The big one!" yelled the light-skinned man as he ran past the other men toward Isaiah. Ben and Isaiah didn't look back; they just ran as fast as they had ever run before. Their hearts were racing and their blood was pumping. Ben slowly came to a stop after running for a couple of blocks. He came to the realization that they knew Isaiah had the money on him. He turned around and began running in the direction Isaiah had gone. Meanwhile, Isaiah was stuck. He had run into a dead end. Every door was locked. Footsteps clapped against puddles in the alley, somehow as loud as the storm, which was brewing above. Isaiah had no choice but to surrender; he turned around and got on his knees. Isaiah showed them the money in his bag and laid the bag down on the cold, wet pavement. He raised his hands in the air and looked at the ground in disbelief. He thought for sure their plan would work. They would make it out and he and Ben would be rich.

How could I be so foolish? Why did I let this happen? I'm smarter than this. Is this God's punishment?

As these thoughts raced through his mind, the white tattooed man approached him, stopping in front of him. He bent over and picked up the bag of money, staring Isaiah in the face and said, "No one steals from The Throne, especially not a kid like you," he said looking down at Isaiah.

Isaiah, insulted by the comment, spit in his face. "You can't tell me shit," he said.

The man wiped the spit from his face and smirked. "You are one stupid boy."

He lifted the barrel of his gun to meet Isaiah's forehead.

BANG!

The shot rang out through the surrounding area. Ben, still sprinting in hopes of meeting Isaiah, heard the shot. He fell to the floor and started to cry. Tears coursed down his face, meeting the creases of his mouth. He yelled, "No, it can't be true!" Smacking the pavement, he stood back up. Benjamin ran even faster to where the shot originated. Running past the dead-end alley, he halted and slowly backed up to get a better view of the alleyway. There, Isaiah lay alone and lifeless. Ben collapsed to his knees, clashing the water on the pavement. He screamed in pure pain as dark clouds above poured down harder on them.

Ben lifted Isaiah's head to see a hole in his forehead. The exit hole on the back of his head began to ooze thick scarlet blood that covered Ben's hands.

He stared in disbelief as rage, hate, pain, sadness, sorrow, and guilt rushed over him. Isaiah's body slowly slipped from Ben's hands and fell onto the ground, smashing his head. Ben felt overwhelmed with grief as he struggled to make sense of what had just taken place. Staring up, Ben began to cry again, yelling as lightning struck, "What good are you? You protect nothing! He praises you every day and you kill him! You are nothing!" Ben screamed until his breath ran out and the veins on his neck were ready to explode. He collapsed onto Isaiah, hugging him and crying. Then, his rage returned as he smashed the wet pavement with his fist.

"No," He cried. "No, no no no." He shook his head as he sat up. His face went serious and he sniffled as the cold rain beat against him. "No!" Benjamin yelled. He hoisted Isaiah onto his back and began jogging to the hospital as the rain started to pick up and come down even harder.

Benjamin had stopped crying and screaming, but he wasn't calm. There was a look in his eyes that no one should ever have; he was gone, lost as though there was no longer a reason to live. His eyes were cold and empty, not looking ahead of himself where he was running but spaced out.

Why am I running? What am I doing? he thought to himself as he neared the hospital.

"I'm going to save Isaiah before he dies," he answered his own thoughts.

He entered the hospital with tears and Isaiah on his back yelling, "Help, help me, please."

No one answered him.

"It's my brother! Please, help me!"

Three hospital assistants snapped their heads around to show him attention. They helped him lower Isaiah's lifeless body onto a stretcher with too much blood on his face to locate the entry wound. They rolled him away as Ben looked on with false hope.

He was so traumatized by the event that he actually believed Isaiah might still be alive. Ben walked over to the seats in the waiting room, unaware of what to do next. The seats were almost full, filled with other exhausted or worried patients. As he waited, he began to recall memories of his life with Isaiah, thinking of all the time they had spent together. A sharp screeching sound brought him back to reality as Ben looked up to see a walker with wheels too old to roll correctly coming into the corridor. An old man with baggy dress pants and a plaid black cap that accentuated his demeanor was behind the walker. He was yelling about not needed a CT scan, while various family members attempted to restrain him from attacking his wife. He continued to yell that she was after his life insurance.

The whole scene for Ben was interrupted when a nurse softly touched his shoulder. He adjusted himself, standing up to look at her properly as she kept her hand on his shoulder. She said in such an understanding and peaceful way, "I'm sorry. He didn't make it."

Ben dropped to his knees once again, turning to the seats and submerging his face into the red and yellow flower-designed cushions covering the wooden chairs.

"Why? He was my only family! It's not true! It can't be. Let me see him!" Ben burst into a hysterical episode of crying and screaming all at once.

The nurse said, "I'm sorry, Sir. Your friend suffered trauma to the head"

She realized this boy was not comprehending her and tried her best to calm him. There was no escaping the fact of what had happened, but Ben could not make sense of it all.

"Please, come with me and answer some questions about what took place," the nurse said as the same three assistants who first helped him walked towards him attempted to guide him.

Ben realized he had no reason left to stay there and took off towards the exit of the hospital back into the pouring rain. From there, he just walked aimlessly through the darkened streets. He felt a hole in his heart, much like the hole in Isaiah's skull. A piece of him had been removed, leaving his soul wounded and incomplete. He walked towards their makeshift shelter, through the pounding rain and blowing winds, furiously swinging at the air, thinking it would help solve problems. He headed towards the Chinese restaurant but suddenly slipped, tripping and falling onto the pavement. He laid on the ground, senseless, his face completely submerged in a rising puddle.

CHAPTER 26

The Throne's throne had been left empty for too long. Several gangs had risen up in defiance of the 21 Dragons. Along with that, the Latin Kings had shown increased aggression against them, leaving more than a warning to stay away from their territory. The 21 Dragons were now held together by the ambitious teens that joined the gang for the status of being a dragon.

Throne had finally returned from his meeting with the professionals with a good deal. Throne had plans to expand his territory further and align with the big leaguers. Attempting to get up to speed, he called a meeting and expected to hear about their progress.

The white tattooed man approached him. "Boss, you're back!"

"Yeah." Throne walked past the man with O-Time, Muscle P, and Frank alongside him.

"Boss, I got news for you," the white man smiled.

"Yeah, I heard. This place is getting out of hand. Those damned Latin Kings killed Mikey and Akkun."

"Well yeah, that too."

Throne turned his head with a snap and a disgusted look on his face. "What do you mean *too*?" Throne gave him the attention he was begging for.

Still smirking, he answered. "We caught two little shit bags stealing from you."

"What do you mean? Who?" Throne asked.

"Well, sorta caught them. One of them got away. But don't worry, we got your money back and we gave one of them a lesson, too. That one that didn't get away and paid for it."

"Who?!" Throne demanded as he felt the rage beginning to build.

"I don't know, two bum ass kids."

Throne clicked his tongue. "Anyone know who stole from me?"

The room was silent until big Arthur stood. "I just got here, too." Arthur said with a ghostly face.

"Art, man, what's up?" Throne dapped Arthur up and hugged him. "Why aren't you at the Costco with that 2am group?"

"I heard what's been happening. I'm needed here."

"So, what's with this shit. Who stole my money?"

"I know. It wasn't just two bums."

Throne leaned in, lifting his shades, understanding the seriousness in Arthur's voice.

"That dummy killed Isaiah and Ben is gone for good," Arthur said with fury as he pointed to the white man with tattoos.

Without a second thought, Throne turned to the white man and put a bullet in his skull. "Damn clown!" Throne kicked the lifeless body as it laid on the floor. "That settles that. Now, we go to war with those kings who want my throne."

The room was not startled. They felt Isaiah had been avenged. Most of them were just relieved they didn't have to account for their slacking while Throne was away. They knew they were in deep and Throne would only be leading them deeper. There was no return.

His most trusted members behind him were unaware of Throne's next move but they were ready. Throne had clearly lost some control but it didn't seem to affect his ego.

"No more nonsense around here. That dumbass killed Isaiah. Shit will be run right from now on. First things first, we get revenge for Mikey and Akkun. Fuck those so-called Kings; the throne belongs to me."

With that, Throne and his men began to prepare for war. They cleaned their guns and prepared their ammo. No one smiled or joked; no one said a word. All that was heard was the sound of guns clicking and ammo locking. Throne went to the bathroom as they were finishing up. From his pocket, he pulled out a small baggie. Inside this bag was a white powder. He removed some with his fingertip and then snorted it off his nail. He cleaned his nose with water and shook himself loose. Then, he returned to O-Time's living room, ready to address his gang. Not everyone associated with 21 Dragons was there. But the core, along with some six or so new members, were ready to fight. They all hopped into two black SUVs and placed masks over their heads.

As the car drove to their destination, they all began to smoke weed and pop pills. They were headed for Aurora in the Chicago Metropolitan Area. As they approached a red light, the two black SUVs lined up with each other. Frank was the driver of one and Art the other. They nodded at each other and waited at the light. They did not realize that there was a group of thirty or so men wearing masks approaching from the back and sides of the vehicles. They opened the doors and shot inside, each masked man bearing an assault rifle. No one was left alive. With one swoop, all of the 21 Dragons were beheaded.

Ben couldn't shake the feeling of abandonment. It was unbearable. All was lost and nothing could be forgotten.

Benjamin woke up. He realized he was inside a storage room and sleeping on two tables. As he awoke and turned, he saw the door was open and there were three men sitting on chairs in the kitchen of the Chinese restaurant.

The old Chinese man must have saved me, Ben thought.

CHAPTER 27

"Sir we were closing in when he slipped and fell; he was recovered by a civilian and brought into the restaurant," one of the field agents said as they waited across the street from the Chinese restaurant. The rain and wind roared at them yet they stood tall, clothed completely in black.

"Prepare to infiltrate on my command," Jason said to them.

The two field agents used hand signals to direct each other to opposite sides of the restaurant. When they were both lined up at the front and back entrance, they responded to Jason. "Copy that, Sir. In position."

CHAPTER 28

As the realization came flooding back that he was alone without Isaiah, Ben attempted to get up, but a sharp pain in his stomach forced him back down.

"Oh, no you don't! No getting away this time." One of the men laughed as he got up from his chair and approached Benjamin.

Ben looked at the young man that approached him, speaking far better English than old man Yu. He was wearing blue scrubs. He had brown hair with golden streaks dyed in, with boxy black prescription glasses. Ben assumed it was the old man's son.

"I'm not talking."

"Progress! You spoke!" He laughed again.

Ben scoffed, turning his head away from him aggressively. As he did, he winced in pain.

The young man sighed and looked at the floor. "Would you at least talk to your hero?"

"My hero?"

"Yes, if it wasn't for them, you would be long dead, still lying in that alleyway. Mr. Yu and his employees, Chang Guo and Fan Linlin, saved you. You almost drowned in that puddle. And since you were passed out, they had to carry you all the way here in the rain."

"Why didn't they just leave me there?" Ben answered, unamused.

"My father is a great man and he recognizes greatness," the young man said with his chest out. "It's not often that he talks about someone like he's talked about you and your friend."

Ben looked past the young man to see a group of two short men and one woman, all with unique and genuine smiles.

Mr. Bai Yu was a very short older man who owned the restaurant that had been supplying Ben with leftover food. Chang Guo was another short man but heavy set and round. He was the chef of the restaurant. Finally, there was Fan Linlin, who stood taller than the two men. She was an elegant yet rather dangerous looking woman.

Ben smiled back at them and waved; he motioned a thank you with his hand. They bowed in response.

"They respect you."

"I'm just a dirty, rotten, homeless boy. Why do they care?"

"Status means nothing to them. What's on the inside matters. They see through the top layer of this world and into the soul of others. They have seen your soul and deemed it worthy of respect, regardless of how it may seem to you."

"Profound stuff."

The young man smiled and scratched the back of his head. "I'm not usually like this. I'm sorry, I got all preachy on you."

"I think I needed a little sermon."

The man smiled again and turned away.

Ben fell back asleep and slept for a little while. His nightmare awoke him to an even scarier reality. Isaiah was gone and he wasn't coming back.

Of course, Benjamin was thankful. How could he not be? Thankful for Mr. Yu's kind actions through their time living in the alley and his continued watch over the boys. Thankful for his son and his kind words and for the staff saving him from drowning in a puddle after knocking himself unconscious. Their hospitality gave him nostalgia of the old days when his foster mother, Grace, would give him all his favorite snacks for school.

Still, Ben felt a gaping hole inside him, which grew every second. Nothing could fix what was broken and Ben no longer had any purpose to keep trying. The nostalgic feeling turned into deep sorrow as he reimagined the beatings and abusive punishments.

Benjamin's head pounded and his chest grew tight—not from the fall, but from trying to process the events that had unfolded just hours prior.

If there was a god, Ben hated him. He would rather be tortured in hell than live in heaven with a merciless god. The wise, old Chinese man meant a lot to Benjamin, but not enough to keep living. When Ben saw his moment, he slipped out of the storage room and past the hallway, through the swinging doors and into the kitchen. There was one man preparing soup for the next day. As the chef was chopping vegetables, he did not notice Ben take a large kitchen knife and walk towards the back exit. The torrential rainfall and aggressive winds set the stage as it grew difficult for Benjamin to think straight.

Adrenaline began to take over his body as he felt raging and intensive hate for himself. The emotions spiraled like a rollercoaster as he felt dejected, maniacal, and disoriented. With the large silver knife from the cook's station, Ben exited the kitchen to the back alley and out into the storm, which had significantly picked up, flushing rain and wind through the large alley passageway. Ben shut the door behind him and stared at the knife in his hands. The night grew darker and the clouds from the rain covered the moon, making it difficult to see. The boy stood against the wind in the rain, his knuckles turning white from the tense grip on the handle. Ben looked at the knife and thought about his future without Isaiah. He gripped the knife with two hands and raised it above his shoulders. He rocked back and forth as he prepared himself. Then, Benjamin screamed and thrust the cold blade down into his abdomen, plunging it through his pale skin. The blood ran from his stomach like water escaping an overflowing swimming pool. He removed the knife from his stomach and dropped it to the ground, splashing into the puddle below him. Ben began stumbling until he collapsed. Clenching himself in pain, he started to cry. He sobbed like a baby—not from the pain of the knife but from the pain of losing Isaiah. Lying in his own blood alone in the alley, he imagined they slept together, finally in peace. Ben stared up at the driving rain until blackness overtook him. The black was endless, as if he were far away in outer space without stars to show him a way out.

Then, slowly, a single white glimmer of light enticed Benjamin's soul and kept him vitalized as he journeyed through the endless black abyss. Nobody to feel, no mind to think, no eyes to see. Only his soul, which tossed through the void like a single grain of sand cast into an ocean of white during a sandstorm. All his soul could do was strive toward the light, opposing the turmoil of darkness.

***